HARD TIMES

PITT SERIES IN RUSSIAN AND EAST EUROPEAN STUDIES

Jonathan Harris, Editor

A NOVEL OF LIBERALS AND RADICALS IN 1860s RUSSIA

HARD TIMES

Vasily Sleptsov

———

Translated by
MICHAEL R. KATZ

Introduction by
WILLIAM C. BRUMFIELD

———

University of Pittsburgh Press

Published by the University of Pittsburgh Press, Pittsburgh, Pa., 15260

Copyright © 2016, University of Pittsburgh Press

All rights reserved

Manufactured in the United States of America

Printed on acid-free paper

10 9 8 7 6 5 4 3 2 1

ISBN 13: 978-0-8229-6422-3

ISBN 10: 0-8229-6422-8

Cataloging-in-Publication data is available from the Library of Congress

Cover art: Detail of Grigoriy Myasoyedov's *Zemstvo Is Having Their Lunch*, 1872. Oil on canvas, 49.2 x 29.1 in.

Cover design by Alex Wolfe

~ for Alya ~

CONTENTS

TRANSLATOR'S PREFACE

———

Michael R. Katz

VASILY SLEPTSOV (1836–1878) WAS A GIFTED RUSSIAN writer and an ardent social reformer. Born in Voronezh, the son of landowning gentry, he was forced to leave the institute in Penza where he had been a student because he had declared himself as a non-believer during a church service. Sleptsov attended medical school at Moscow University but didn't complete the course. He went off to Yaroslavl to launch his career as an actor, but that too was unsuccessful. He returned to Moscow, where he briefly held a post in government service. During the early 1860s Sleptsov organized what was to become Russia's most famous commune in St. Petersburg, based on the principles of Charles Fourier and N. G. Chernyshevsky; that social experiment, however, was beset with numerous problems and lasted only a short time.

When Sleptsov set out in 1860 to collect folk songs, fairy tales, and proverbs for the Society of Lovers of Russian Philology, he became genuinely interested in the plight of the common people. He undertook an investigation of the conditions of Russia's peasants and workers during the difficult years following the emancipation of the serfs. He also became associated with a radical circle grouped around the salon of Countess Elizabeth Salias de Tournemir, a publisher and minor writer who was known under the pseudonym Evgeniia Tur.

Sleptsov began writing stories for several journals including the *Contemporary*, where he published his novella *Hard Times* [*Trudnoe vremya*] in 1865. The work enjoyed remarkable popularity during the remainder of that decade. It dealt with complicated political issues that were in the forefront of popular attention: the emancipation of the serfs, related administrative and judicial reforms, political repression, the growth of radicalism, and the movement for women's rights. Few Russian novels became the subject of such heated debate. Sleptsov's characters were endlessly discussed, analyzed, dissected, and then reassembled in the political image of its various commentators. The main question posed by the novel was whether Russia should follow the path of liberal reform or radical change. Since the author had personal knowledge of the radical movement, he was able to incorporate that into his fiction, thus providing a sober appraisal of a turbulent decade. Critical reactions to the novel were predictably diverse and extraordinarily impassioned.

One year after his novel was published, Sleptsov was arrested for his political activities and his association with Dmitrii Karakozov, the man who later attempted to assassinate Tsar Alexander II. Sleptsov spent only seven weeks incarcerated in Peter-Paul Fortress, released after his mother interceded, but he was placed under police surveillance for the rest of his life. Although his works were widely read and discussed during the decade of the 1860s, his popularity soon began to decline. A novel titled *A Good Man* was left unfinished at the time of his death in 1878.

Hard Times takes place during the summer of 1863; that is, two years after the emancipation. The plot is as follows: a radical intellectual, Riazanov, arrives at the estate of his university acquaintance Shchetinin, who is married and settled into the role of an enlightened landowner enacting reforms on his own estate. The two friends engage in a series of arguments during which the radical friend attempts to demolish the liberal's belief in gradual social progress through reform. Under the influence of Riazanov's opinions, Shchetinin's wife can no longer tolerate her husband's ineffective liberalism. She decides to abandon him and her conventional role on his estate, and seeks emotional and moral support from Riazanov. But Riazanov rejects her advances; she perseveres and decides to leave the countryside for St. Petersburg to join the ranks of "new people" and to serve the radical cause anyway.

Hard Times presents a critique of major Russian institutions: schools, courts of law, constitutions, and bills of rights, all subjected to scrutiny through the eyes of colorful minor characters. It also provides detailed vignettes of peasant life and Russian customs, as the main characters travel from the host's manor house to the local village, then to a district meeting of official arbiters (a new institution), and finally through the province observing local mediators attempting to adjudicate disputes between landowners and peasants.

Sleptsov had an uncanny ability to render his characters' speech in natural, yet dramatic form. The dialogue is substantive yet conversational, the language both colloquial and informal in tone, with frequent off-the-cuff remarks, humorous asides, popular sayings, songs, sarcastic utterances, and flashes of anger.

The author has created convincing characters who are neither heroes nor villains: he manages to avoid the romanticism of Turgenev's novels, especially evident in his portrait of the nihilist Bazarov, who succumbs to romantic love in *Fathers and Children* (1862); or the utopian idealism of Chernyshevsky's "new people" and his "extraordinary man" Rakhmetov in *What Is to Be Done?* (1863); or the biting political satire and caricatures of the radicals as portrayed by Dostoevsky in his novel *Devils* (1872).

It is for all these reasons and others that I decided to translate Sleptsov's *Hard Times*. I selected the edition published by Khudozhestvennaya literatura (Moscow, 1979): V. A. Sleptsov, *Izbrannoe* [Selected works], edited by M. L. Semanova, 281–431.

I wish to express my deepest appreciation to my colleague and friend William Brumfield, professor of Slavic studies at Tulane University, the foremost Western scholar on the life and works of Vasily Sleptsov. I am very grateful to him for suggesting this project and for agreeing to write an introduction to this translation. And I am indebted to Lecturer Emerita Aleksandra Baker, known better to the world as Alya, who has been a steadfast supporter and collaborator in many of my translations. Needless to say, any remaining errors or infelicities are my own.

INTRODUCTION

Getting through Hard Times

VASILY SLEPTSOV AND HIS RADICAL HAMLET

———

William C. Brumfield

VASILY SLEPTSOV IS A RARE PHENOMENON IN RUSSIAN literature, a social activist who was able to translate the issues that concerned him into works of literary value. His writings, both fictional as well as nonfictional, were suffused with a sense of the social and political realities particular to the 1860s, that thoroughly politicized decade in Russia. In his person as well as in his works, Sleptsov epitomized the engaged intellectual atmosphere of the "era of great reforms" that followed the abolition of serfdom in 1861.

In his novel *Hard Times*,[1] Sleptsov brought a sympathy for the radical movement into a fictional setting whose characters examine their relations in a constantly evolving social and emotional milieu. The longing for a new life within the languorous setting of a country estate anticipates much in the mature work of Anton Chekhov,

———

1. An extended analysis of Sleptsov's novel is provided in William C. Brumfield, "Sleptsov Redivivus," in *California Slavic Studies* 9 (1976), 27–70. A monographic study of Sleptsov is provided in the same author's *Sotsial'nyi proekt v russkoi literature XIX-ogo veka* (Moscow: Izd. "Tri kvadrata," 2009).

———

who is quoted as saying: "Sleptsov taught me, better than most, to understand the Russian *intelligent* [intellectual, member of the intelligentsia] and my own self as well."[2]

Sleptsov's biography is both revealing and contradictory as a portrait of his times. He was born on July 17, 1836, in Voronezh. Both of his parents had respectable nobility credentials, a fact that separated him from other socially engaged writers of the 1860s. His mother was descended from Polish and Baltic nobility, while his father was of Russian noble lineage with a number of highly placed relatives in Moscow.

In 1837 the family moved to Moscow, where it remained for the next eleven years. The father was now chronically ill and family tensions were exacerbated by his parents' disapproval of Sleptsov's choice of a Polish bride. Although Vasily was a precocious student, his Moscow education was interrupted in 1849 when the family relocated to an inherited estate in Saratov Province. Conditions there were so primitive that Vasily was sent to the Noblemen's Institute in Penza, but he returned to the estate in 1851 following his father's death.

This peripatetic, unstable existence seems to have permanently marked Sleptsov's life. He returned to Moscow and to university life in 1853, but his medical studies were superseded by his love of the theater and ballet. In 1856 he married a ballet dancer, who died the following year. In 1858 he remarried; he and his second wife (the daughter of Tver gentry) had two children. Having settled his family at his Saratov estate in 1860, he separated from his wife and returned to Moscow.

---

2. Chekhov's comment was recorded in a conversation with the writer Maksim Gorkii, who conveyed it in a letter written in late February 1912 to D. N. Ovsyaniko-Kulykovskii. First published in *M. Gor'kii. Materialy i issledovaniia*, vol. I (Leningrad: Akademiia nauk, 1934), 284. Chekhov not only knew Sleptsov's work but also was friends with two women who had been closely acquainted with Sleptsov: Lidiia Maklakova and Liubov Vorontsova. The former, better known under her literary pseudonym Nelidova, lived with Sleptsov for his last three years and wrote a novel, *Na maloi zemle* (unpublished), about their life together.

There Sleptsov launched his career as a writer among a group of "radicals" grouped around the salon of Countess Elizabeth Salias de Tournemir.[3] In 1861 her journal, *Russian Speech*, published his first significant work, "Vladimirka and the Kliazma," an engagingly idiosyncratic travel narrative that gathered ethno-linguistic material and doubled as an exposé of corruption in the construction of the Moscow-Nizhny Novgorod Railroad. While working at the journal, Sleptsov also made the acquaintance of the writer Nikolai Leskov, who subsequently became an implacable enemy.

The success of this work drew the attention of Nikolai Nekrasov, a renowned poet, critic, and editor of the leading intellectual journal the *Contemporary*. Nekrasov commissioned another exposé from Sleptsov. His subsequent "Letters from Ostashkov" (1862), a jaundiced look at the town's reformist pretentions, launched his most productive period. Having moved to St. Petersburg in late 1862, Sleptsov became one of the most frequent contributors to the revived *Contemporary*. Of particular note was his publication in 1863 and 1864 of a series of brilliantly crafted short stories that subsequently attracted the attention of Tolstoy, Turgenev, and Chekhov.

Sleptsov's most publicized and controversial activity was the founding of what was subsequently known as the Znamenskaia or Sleptsov commune. In and of itself a commune was not that unusual a phenomenon in St. Petersburg or Moscow during the 1860s. Indeed, it seems in retrospect that its most remarkable feature was the fact that it received so much attention, from both the police and the public.

Sleptsov was familiar with Nikolai Chernyshevsky's recent novel *What Is to Be Done?* (especially its description of the heroine's

---

3.   Perhaps the foremost woman writer of her generation, the countess wrote under the pseudonym Evgeniia Tur. A section of her four-volume novel was translated into English by Michael Katz: *Antonina* (Evanston, IL: Northwestern University Press, 1996).

model commune for seamstresses).[4] Furthermore, he himself was much involved in efforts to provide employment for women with no means to support themselves. A communal living arrangement à la Chernyshevsky would be the logical extension of these efforts. And it is known that Sleptsov was at least superficially familiar with the theories of Fourier and was particularly interested in his practical ideas on the formation of a "phalanstery."

Organization began in August 1863, but internal bickering and ideological dissent among the commune's members, as well as poor financial management, led to its disbanding after only a few months.

By the end of 1864, however, Sleptsov had begun work on what was to become his magnum opus, *Hard Times*. This short novel was announced in the December issue of *Contemporary* and appeared in installments during the following year. It was to catapult Sleptsov to the height of his literary career, and it remains a monument not only to the writer but also to the decade it reflects. Few works from that era provoked such a storm of partisan reaction. In essence *Hard Times* dealt with the fundamental issue confronting prerevolutionary Russian society: What is to be done with a system facing massive, perhaps insurmountable, social problems—a course of work and reform within the system or rejection of the entire system and, eventually, revolution?

The success of Sleptsov's work in 1865 was soon brutally interrupted. On April 4, 1866, Dmitrii Karakozov—a former student and member of an extreme faction of a radical circle—made an unsuccessful attempt on the life of Alexander II. The ensuing reaction not only crushed the remnants of the circle but also had a considerable impact on Russian intellectual life.

On April 30, 1866, Sleptsov was arrested under suspicion of radical sympathies and taken to Peter-Paul Fortress. Most of those arrested were released after a few weeks (seven in Sleptsov's

---

4. The phrase "what is to be done?" occurs frequently during this period as an echo of Chernyshevsky's title.

case), but even such a relatively short confinement had serious effects.

Something seems to have fractured in Sleptsov's life. For a few years he continued to be active in Petersburg intellectual life—particularly in the cause of women's equality. However, he found it increasingly difficult to devote attention to his writing, and his career floundered, despite Nekrasov's best intentions. In his personal life, though, he managed to find lasting and devoted love in the companionship of his common-law wife. His health problems took an alarming turn. In 1877 the impoverished Sleptsov journeyed to the Caucasus to seek respite from the pain, but to no avail. Evidence suggests that he suffered from intestinal cancer.

Sleptsov, in seriously weakened condition, returned to his mother's estate near Serdobsk in March 1878. He died two weeks later after a long period of agony. Plans to have him buried at Petersburg's prominent Volkovo Cemetery were abandoned for lack of funds. He was interred in the Serdobsk village cemetery, its small church surrounded by the steppe.

One constant in Sleptsov's combination of literature and social activism was his engagement in the movement for women's emancipation. No other Russian writer, Chernyshevsky not excepted, portrayed the issues of feminism, the background of frustration, the restraints of convention as cogently as he did. In *Hard Times* as well as in his feuilletons, Sleptsov repeatedly championed the cause of equality for women. In this respect he has much in common with the Norwegian playwright Henrik Ibsen, whose plays, such as *A Doll's House*, resemble *Hard Times* in their portrayal of the heroine's revolt against her bourgeois, or gentry, milieu.

Yet just what sort of radical was Sleptsov? He certainly was an opponent of what he saw as ineffectual attempts to patch a leaky social and political order, and he was consistent in exposing (as far as censorship would allow) the many abuses and grave social problems confronting Russia during the 1860s. Sleptsov was not, however, a doctrinaire ideologue, nor was he an active revolutionary.

Radical activists in the 1860s had not yet formulated a concrete plan for political revolution. With the disenchantment of hopes for a transformation of Russian society following the emancipation of the serfs, few "critically thinking individuals" of that era were able to visualize the means by which meaningful social and political change would occur.

Sleptsov, like others of radical persuasion, could only work for a change in social attitudes and continued to reject the possibility of reform within the existing regime. This approach can best be characterized as "classic" nihilism, a term that, in its political and social meaning, originated from and was particularly well suited to the 1860s. Such a "nihilistic" approach served Sleptsov well in *Hard Times*, but his eventual search for a positive alternative led only to disillusionment, frustration, and literary paralysis. Like his protagonist in *Hard Times*, Sleptsov fell into the grip of the "Hamlet syndrome."

As Sleptsov's most significant work, the novel ensured his reputation as a critical realist while igniting a polemical response that lasted until the revolution. Few works in the history of Russian literature have been the subject of such heated debate or have had their main characters so discussed, analyzed, dissected, and reassembled in the political image of the commentator. That such a reaction should have occurred is understandable in light of then prevailing attitudes toward the function and duty of literary criticism to serve as a vehicle for social and political comment.

The novel is well suited to such attitudes, since it deals with the most volatile issue confronting educated Russian society after the Emancipation: Should Russia follow the path of liberal reform or that of radical change? In the figure of the novel's protagonist, Riazanov, Sleptsov presents a portrait of the radical intelligentsia during one of its most turbulent and crucial states of development. Nowhere is the politicized, radical intellectual depicted with greater sympathy and yet with so little idealization; nowhere are the attitudes of the "thinking proletariat" (Dmitry Pisarev's phrase) displayed more cogently.[5] Sleptsov's nihilist is as important and as controversial as Turgenev's hero Bazarov for any attempt to recapture the spirit of the sixties. Both represent the Russian intelligentsia's groping search for "the real day."[6]

Since *Hard Times* is so deeply rooted in the issues and events of that decade, it would be well to review the situation at that time. The action takes place in the summer of 1863, some two years after the Emancipation Proclamation was signed by Alexander II. The success (or failure) of the Emancipation, as well as the reforms connected with it, had become the focus of intense debate. Liberals welcomed the reforms and felt that the only path to progress lay in gradual change, supervised by a strong centralized government.

On the radical side, Chernyshevsky, in particular, was quite vocal in his opposition to the terms of the serfs' liberation. As early as 1858 and 1859, during the formative stages of Emancipation policy, he had consistently argued for a reduction of redemption payments and for a redistribution of land within the framework of the peasant commune. The land reform of 1861 was, for Chernyshevsky as for Sleptsov, a deal between landowners and the state that preserved the rights and many privileges of the gentry, while leaving the peasant to fend for himself under extremely unfavorable conditions. Despite an initial euphoria with the concept of emanci-

5. The phrase "thinking proletariat" was coined by the critic Dmitry Pisarev in his article "Novyi tip" ("the new type"), first published in the intellectual journal *Russkoe slovo* 1865, no. 10. Republished in D. I. Pisarev, *Sobraniie sochinenii v 4-kh tomakh* (Moscow: GIKhL, 1956), 12–24. Pisarev's article presented an extended analysis of the characters in Chernyshevsky's novel *What Is to Be Done?*

6. In the early 1860s the phrase "the real day" (*nastoiashchii den'*) gained currency in Russian social criticism as a covert reference to impending fundamental social change in Russia. The first published use can be dated to the radical critic Nikolai Dobrolyubov's widely read essay "When Will the Real Day Come?" ("Kogda zhe pridet nastoiashchii den'?"), published in the intellectual journal *Russkii vestnik* in 1860. The essay was an extended commentary on Ivan Turgenev's novel *On the Eve*.

pation and its possibilities, the eventual formulation of Emancipation policy was seen as faulty, impractical, and unjust.

The ephemeral hopes of certain radicals for a general revolution, based on peasant disturbances after the Emancipation, failed to materialize. A series of mysterious fires in Petersburg and various towns along the Volga during 1862 only served to strengthen the government's policy of repression, as did the Polish rebellion of 1863. As a result of the latter, oppositional tendencies among the liberal gentry evaporated, while radicals lacking coherent organization detested liberals and feuded among themselves. It is these "hard times" that form the historical background of Sleptsov's novel.

In addition, the issue of women's emancipation—psychological, mental, and legal—occupies a prominent position in determining the relations between Sleptsov's characters.[7] In *Hard Times* the author applied his commitment to the "woman question" to form a thematic line that rivals the contest between the liberal estate owner (Shchetinin) and his radical acquaintance (Riazanov).

Such is the work's base—the events and issues that constitute its theme and motivate its action. Its artistic implementation is deceptively simple: there is little plot development, and, despite the possibility for a *ménage à trois*, the love interest is redirected. Instead, the work is oriented toward development of its two major themes, the exposé of liberal gradualism and the right of a woman to determine her own future. To this end it is heavily dependent on lively dialogue—witty "confrontations" among its three leading characters.

Limited to the events that produce an estrangement between Shchetinina and her husband, the plot structure is a sparse frame

---

7. In literature the issue of women's emancipation had already appeared prominently in George Sand's novel *Jacques* (1833) and Alexander Herzen's *Who Is to Blame?*, first published in the journal *Otechestvennye zapiski* in 1845–1846 and republished as a book in 1847. Both works were widely known among Russian writers and intellectuals.

for the considerable thematic load placed upon it. It is the dialogue, at once substantive and conversational, that sustains the novel. The language itself is colloquial and informal, with frequent use of particles, verbs without subjects, and numerous colloquial expressions. And then there are passages that illustrate Sleptsov's uncanny ability to convey peasant speech. Off-the-cuff remarks, humorous or sarcastic interjections, flashes of anger, an abrupt shift from one scene to the next—these devices vary the pace and propel the plot forward, while narrative intrusions are so rare that the work reads like a play. It is not surprising that Konstantin Stanislavsky, in a letter to Vladimir Nemirovich-Danchenko, suggested that, with a few modifications, *Hard Times* would be suitable for staging.

Despite Sleptsov's sympathy with Riazanov's political views and Shchetinina's break with her past, the characters are treated with equanimity. All have their limitations. The landowner Shchetinin's emotions are often portrayed as sympathetically as those of the other characters. It is a measure of Sleptsov's success that each of his three personages was in turn designated by contemporary critics as the central, positive figure, the designation depending on the critic's political bias. By the same token, each took his or her share of critical abuse.

Yet any treatment of the literary significance of *Hard Times* must eventually lead to a discussion of Riazanov. In him there is a mingling of two seemingly contradictory images of the Russian literary hero—the superfluous man and the man of action. Riazanov, as a superfluous man, represents a revolution defeated, an activist transformed into a cynic (or realist), drained of emotion and unwilling to respond to the feelings of a woman who loves him—and to whom he is attracted. In a word, a Russian Hamlet. Riazanov as an activist, on the other hand, is something of a professional radical, a writer (probably a political essayist), and his views are conditioned by a sociopolitical, materialist view of history in which the flawed existing order must be overturned.

Lacking the programmatic answers of Chernyshevsky's *What Is to Be Done?* Sleptsov leaves his protagonist suspended in uncertainty.

Nature, then, is called upon to suggest the larger forces at work. For *Hard Times* is suffused with the presence of nature's elemental force—not in the lyrical tone of Turgenev's *Fathers and Children*, with its symbolism of reconciliation and continuity—but a harsher, more elemental force. Through it a larger background is created, one that reflects the atmosphere of ennui and tension prevalent in *Hard Times*. A half century following its publication, war and revolution would destroy the gentry milieu described in the novel, the same setting that nurtured Sleptsov and to which he returned shortly before his death. Although Sleptsov could not possibly have predicted the extent of the cataclysm in *Hard Times*, he has certainly succeeded in conveying a sense of the gathering storm.

HARD TIMES

—

Vasily Sleptsov

CHAPTER I

———

IT WAS SUMMER, VERY EARLY SUMMER. A COACHMAN was driving along a country road, carrying a traveler in a cart, a troika.[1]

The road went across a field, through meadows and ravines, and led to a forest. They entered the forest. It was getting toward evening.

"Is it much further?" asked the traveler.

"Not far."

"How far?"

"Very close. As soon as we leave the forest, we'll be there."

The coachman stopped the horses, climbed down, walked around the cart, tightened the saddle girth, adjusted the shaft bow, and climbed in again; taking up the reins, he shouted to the horses: "Gee up! Not far!"

The cart bounced over tree roots; suddenly a damp, strong-smelling freshness could be felt in the air. The traveler took off his cap, wiped his face with his handkerchief, and stared ahead attentively.

———

1. Sleptsov indicates that the coachman is a "free" man, liberated from serfdom.

Here and there rays of the reddening sun raced incessantly through a scanty grove of oaks and hazels; birds flitted among treetops. The forest was thinning out, becoming sparser and sparser; all at once the sun appeared above the shrubbery, the horses turned sharply to the right, and the cart suddenly arrived at the edge of a daunting precipice along which snaked the road, all pitted, worn, and strewn with small stones. The horses halted. . . .

One could see ahead about twenty versts from this place.[2] Below, under the precipice, was a river dotted with little islands. It flowed down from green meadows, thickly overgrown with sparse curly bushes; it wound around and vanished into the reeds, then shimmered again in the distance, and finally disappeared completely beyond some distant blue lakes. Beyond the opposite riverbank stretched hayfields, grain fields, and small villages. Closer, over to the right, stood a larger village, reaching to a church; both sides of the road were lined with flower and vegetable gardens, barns, and old blackened haystacks. On the right, in a large garden, up on a hillock, stood the manor house. Down below, beneath the hill, the sound of a water mill could be heard.

"What a place!" the traveler said aloud.

"It's a wet spot," the coachman replied. "Some years it makes lots of hay," he added a little later and began descending, urging on the horses: "Careful!"

The traveler surveyed the surroundings; the horses kept slipping and stumbling; without turning around, the coachman asked: "Are you related to our Aleksandr Vasil'ich?"

"No."

"So then, you're their guest?"

"Yes, indeed."

"Nice. And you're in the civil service?"

"No, I'm not."

The coachman turned around.

"Then who are you?"

---

2. About thirteen miles.

"A priest's son."

"Hmm. Yes, yes, yes."

The coachman remained silent for a while, then said pensively: "There are lots of seminary rats like you these days."

"Enough."

"Enough, enough," the coachman said, nodding his head. "Well, and what'll you do next, my friend? Do you plan to ask him to make you a clerk?"

"I have business of my own."

"Yes. Your business of your own. . . . Gee up! You devils! You'll be the death of me! Hey, hey, hey!"

The horses took off, the cart swung first to one side, and then to the other; next, leaping over hummocks, it flew down the road toward the village.

The first thing that caught the traveler's eye was a hut covered in new wooden siding with a porch, standing all alone in a meadow; there was a blue sign over the entrance with white letters: "Local Government."[3] Right there, next to this building, under an awning, was some firefighting equipment: pipes, barrels, hooks, and so forth. Hens wandered around in the road, a piglet squealed as it jumped out from under the wheels, and a peasant hurriedly removed his cap and shook his head. . . .

"Hey, you miserable creatures!" the coachman shouted at his horses; the cart rumbled over a bridge, raised a cloud of dust in the courtyard, and then stopped next to the annex.

A man of average height wearing a coat stood on the porch; thrusting his hands into his pockets, he stared intently at the traveler.

"Is Aleksandr Vasil'ich at home?" the new arrival asked.

"Nope. No one's home," the man replied. "Are you from the district police?" he asked, approaching the cart and inclining his ear.

"No, I'm not; I'm here on my own. Will Aleksandr Vasil'ich be back soon?"

---

3. The *volost'* was the smallest administrative division in tsarist Russia.

"He didn't go far with the mistress, only about twelve versts,[4] to see Mr. Ushakov. They'll be back by this evening. And just who might you be?"

"Me? A friend of his. He knows: he was expecting me."

"Ah! Yes, indeed. I know, sir. Welcome! I'll have your things brought in. . . . Mr. Riazanov?"

"Yes."

"Well, yes. We were expecting you . . . of course. . . ."

"And where should I get settled in the meantime?"

"We've prepared a room for you here in the annex, but right now, I tell you, there's such a commotion going on: the women are fussing . . . all sorts of rags . . . devil take them! No, it's impossible. . . ."

The traveler became thoughtful. "What shall I do?"

"Here's what: in the meantime go into the study. Why not? No problem. This way, please. And I'll . . . Hey! Who's there? Steward! Call someone!"

"No, Ivan Stepanych, there's no need to shout," said the steward, who was approaching in a long heavy peasant's coat and large boots, crossing the courtyard slowly and serenely. "No one's here—it's quitting time. Everyone's gone to the village," he added with a wave of his arm; drawing close to the cart, he began examining the horses. "Are they from Anuchinsky?"[5] he asked the coachman.

"Yes," he replied without looking up.

"Ah, those damned folks!" Ivan Stepanych said in irritation. "As soon as the master leaves, you can't sniff 'em out even with hunting dogs."

"Please, don't go to any trouble," said the traveler. "I'll carry my own things."

"Oh, no. How can you? Steward! Come now, friend, take his suitcase, and I'll bring his traveling bag and his pillow. This way, please!"

---

4. About eight miles.

5. A district in far eastern Siberia.

The steward rested his hat on the porch, picked up the suitcase, and carried it inside.

The house was old-fashioned, one story with a belvedere, but it had been recently remodeled and renovated. Various incongruities and inconveniences, typical of old country houses, had been eliminated for the most part with the help of some additions and alterations, which, although they'd achieved their goal, had, on the other hand, deprived the structure of its typical nature and, as was apparent, completely distorted its previous character. It was a long, poorly whitewashed building; both ends had been fitted out with unwieldy extensions and terraces. In one place a window had been boarded up, while in another, a new window had been inserted. From the first glance it was clear that the new builder had one goal in mind—comfort; he cared little for symmetry or the appearance of the house altogether.

There was no one in the entrance hall or, for that matter, in the entire house; only the setting sun, shining directly into the broad windows of the living room, ran in a crimson streak through a series of deserted rooms. Inside the house, even more than outside, were fresh traces of the recent reform: new doors, new wallpaper, and partitions inserted, apparently, in the name of coziness; in some places there was new furniture; and finally, there were a few fashionable lamps with the pungent smell of kerosene. In spite of all this, in spite of the undeniable improvements that had been carried out over everything, absolutely everything, there hovered another, indelible impression: low ceilings, broad tile stoves, even the dimensions and disposition of the rooms—all clearly indicated that one could burn down old houses of this sort, but they could never be remodeled.

The guest walked quietly through the whole house, pausing silently in various rooms; then he returned to the entrance hall. A large oak-frame mirror hung there in a pier; new high-back oak chairs stood on either side; in the corner there was an oak coat rack; but a wide, awkward, newly painted shelf remained along the wall.

"Where shall I go?" the guest inquired of the man escorting him.

"This way, to the study. If you please! Would you like some tea? Or to freshen up? Right away."

The guest remained alone; he sat down on the sofa and looked around the room: there were bookcases, a fireplace, papers, and newspapers on the table, netting on the windows, a garden below, and the sun setting beyond the garden. . . .

Some boots creaked in the dining room.

"Well, sir, some tea, perhaps?"

The coachman stood in the doorway, scratching the back of his head, wondering what to do next. Just then Ivan Stepanych came in carrying a washbasin.

"Ah, what miserable creatures, damn them! There's no water. I sent the coachman to fetch some. Ugh, what people!"

"Why are you fussing? There's plenty of time."

"No, that's not the point, it's . . . it's simply unheard of! They're so spoiled. It's too much to bear! Would you care to wash up?"

While the guest did so, Ivan Stepanych kept talking: "Soap? Right here! . . . It won't be long now. . . . They never stay there for long. He's not their kind of man . . . this rudeness, you know. . . . He's a landowner, in a word, a landowner. . . . 'Hey, Vanka, bring in a pipe!' Here, sir! The master . . . yes, the master. . . . He hates all those machines. . . . Mar'ia Nikolavna doesn't like to visit him."

"Who's Mar'ia Nikolavna?"

"Why, she's Aleksandr Vasil'ich's wife."

"Yes, I forgot her name."

"Yes, of course. A wonderful lady, well brought up. Aren't many like her around. I say, why live here, really? It's the hinterland: devil take it!"

"So why do you live here?"

"Me? It's my job. I'd be glad to live elsewhere."

"What do you do here?"

"I'm Aleksandr Vasil'ich's clerk. There's some soap left on your beard. Lower! Lower! His clerk. . . . Yes, indeed—his clerk! What the hell? For goodness' sake! What do I do? Someone's calf wanders into the vegetable garden, causes a half-kopeck's worth of damage trespassing; but it leaves behind twenty-five kopecks' worth of manure. A court case! An arbitrator . . . decide the matter. Self-government, he sez. . . . They write in these here papers: the good common sense of the people. . . . Those devils! Indeed. . . . All these schools. . . . To hell with 'em. . . . Here's a towel. I sez to Aleksandr Vasil'ich. . . . Want some tea?"

"No, not now. I'll wait for them."

"Fine, wait for them! I sez to Aleksandr Vasil'ich: give 'em a beating!"

"And what does he say?"

"What's he say? Always the same thing—from the newspapers: benevolence. Oh, good Lord! That's the story! Freedom, he sez. No, there it is, freedom! A few days ago some state-owned peasants came to ask if they could register as our peasants and so on; well, he sez; they've heard, they say, that life here's good. Huh? Freedom? Good common sense? No, damn it, they don't have any common sense, and no one's thought it through. . . . Another person, you know, as soon as he gets all riled up, would show 'em what benevolence was all about."

Just then the steward appeared in the next room, shifting his weight from one leg to the other. He stood at a distance looking in from the doorway, clearing his throat.

"He seems to want to speak with you," said the guest.

"Ah, yes; the steward. Right away. No, I tell you, it's a misfortune. I must go register. Won't you keep yourself busy somehow? Here are some newspapers: *Moscow News, Northern Post.* . . . You know French? *Le Nord, Les Débats.*[6] Feel free to read! Wait a moment, steward!"

"Right away. Or, perhaps you want a magazine?"

"Fine. I'll have a look," said the guest, sitting down at the desk.

"Go on! Read!" the clerk shouted as he left.

---

6. *Le Nord* [*The North*] was published in Belgium and was subsidized by the Russian government; *Les Débats* [*The Debates*] was a Parisian newspaper.

Left alone, the guest yawned and began skimming through some newspapers, but they were all old issues, same for the magazines; he turned the pages reluctantly, lethargically. On the table there also happened to be some Russian and French brochures, mixed in with information from the arbitration meeting and some unattractive copies of *Agronomische Zeitung*,[7] various bills, accounts, household matters, crudely jotted down in pencil. Besides, from traces of flies on the yellowed paper, it was obvious that they'd been written a long time ago and were scattered about from negligence. On the wall next to the desk were hooks hung with decrees, official instructions, penalty tariffs for trespassing damage to crops, and other items of this nature. Open boxes of papers sat on chairs; on the sofa lay the uncut latest issue of *Journal d'agriculture pratique*[8] and a dog collar. The guest stretched out in an armchair and rested his foot under the table on a large pile of *Russian Gazette*s. The unopened packages went sliding all across the floor. After kicking them back under the table with his foot, he stood up and paced the room. Meanwhile it was growing so dark that it was already difficult to make out several photographic portraits hanging over the sofa: the faces were all familiar. The guest grimaced; turning away, he unexpectedly caught a glimpse of his own face in a mirror. . . . He shuddered—and began examining his image: in the dark glass he saw the dim reflection of a gaunt figure with an emaciated face and an immobile gaze. The guest lay down on the sofa and closed his eyes.

A quarter of an hour passed. Suddenly a commotion erupted in the house. Someone ran into the entrance hall carrying a candle, dogs started barking, and an open horse-drawn carriage drove up to the porch; two people were sitting in it: a man and a woman. Their voices could be heard outside:

"Who is it?"

"I don't know."

"Why didn't you ask?"

---

7.   *Agronomical Newspaper* (Ger.).

8.   *Journal of Practical Agriculture* (Fr.).

Right after this a young, fair-haired man entered the study and paused in perplexity.

"I wouldn't have recognized you," said the guest, approaching and extending his hand.

"Ah, it's you, Riazanov! I'd begun to think you weren't coming. Well, well. How are you? Bring some light! You're so thin, so very thin! Sit down; I want to get a good look at you. Let's have some tea!"

"Fine."

"Hurry up, bring the samovar!" cried the master; then he embraced his guest and sat him down on the sofa. "So, tell me, how are things in Piter?[9] What's happening there?"

"Everything's fine, thank heavens. They send you regards."

"What nonsense! Who sends me regards? I don't even know a dog there."

"So then, what do you need to know?"

"Well, at least tell me this: why didn't you write? Not a word in the last three years! Aren't you ashamed? Huh?" said the master, sitting down on the sofa next to his guest. He asked him again: "Aren't you ashamed?"

"No, friend, I'm not. What's the use of writing? No one writes letters nowadays."

"Oh, you! And this is after you call yourself a writer," the master said with a laugh.

"So what if I am? Does that mean I'm supposed to compose letters to you?"

"Compose? You could just write about how things are."

"What a strange fellow you are! And what if there's nothing to write?"

"Tell me, friend. You think I don't know what's going on there?"

"Well, if you know, then what else do you need? Don't you read the newspapers?"

---

9. An affectionate Russian diminutive for the city of St. Petersburg.

"But it's not the same."

"No, it's precisely what you need to know; it's not right for you to know any more."

"You're missing the point," said the host, standing up and laughing. "The devil only knows what I'm asking about. A man's just arrived, and here I am talking about literature. How about some tea? Wait, I'll light some candles. I'm really very glad, and that's why," he said striking a match, "that's why I'm getting so mixed up. Forgive me, please!"

"That's all right," replied the guest, trying to make himself comfortable on the sofa. "It's even a good thing that you're getting mixed up."

The candles flared up little by little lighting up the green walls with their dark portraits and the shapes of these two friends: one— lean, dark, with long scanty hair, and a wedge-shaped beard (Riazanov)—uncomfortably curved, lying on the sofa, and seriously regarding the other—a fair-haired, fresh young man (Shchetinin),[10] who suddenly and unexpectedly became pensive and motionless, still holding a burning match in his hand.

"Why so pensive?" the guest asked at last.

"Who? Me? No, it's nothing. Just so," replied Shchetinin; he sighed and walked across the room. Then he turned sharply toward Riazanov; thrusting his hands into his jacket pockets, he said: "You know what this is all about? You live here alone, seeing no one, and somehow you fall into a trance; then all of sudden you hear some word, just one word, and all of a sudden the old yeast starts to rise."

The guest remained silent. Shchetinin paced from corner to corner three times, paused again in front of the guest, and started speaking: "No, I'm glad to see you, very glad!" He extended his hand to the guest, shook it warmly, and sat down next to him, putting his feet up on the sofa. "Well, now, begin! Tell

---

10. Shchetinin's name is derived from the Russian word *shchetina*, bristles (of a brush) or stubble (of a beard).

me how things really are with you there. You've grown so thin, my friend!"

"What's to be done?" the guest answered with indifference.

"Tell me this," Shchetinin said in a low voice, moving closer. "Explain why you've really come here."

"What do you mean why? You knew that I wanted to recover in the fresh air. And you were the one who invited me."

"I did invite you, but I thought you might have some other purpose besides breathing fresh air."

"No, nothing else. Besides getting to see you."

Shchetinin looked his guest intently in the eye. "Are you telling the truth?"

"Hmm. Why ask me that? If I don't want to tell you, I won't, no matter how much you ask or direct your penetrating gaze at me."

"I thought you'd tell me."

"In vain. . . . And if you really wanted to know why I've come, you could try to find out yourself, trying to get it out of me more shrewdly: initiate conversations about certain topics and take note, or else you could get me drunk. There are so many different ways. . . . Perhaps you'll find out."

"Well, there you go again! I see you're still the same!"

"Yes, indeed, my friend."

"Aren't you fed up with it all?"

"What's to be done? Perhaps, I am, but there's nothing to be done; you can't remake yourself."

"I've remade myself here."

"You have?"

"Yes. Are you surprised by that?"

"No, not really. Where's your wife?"

"She's not feeling well and has probably gone to bed. Oh, yes! I completely forgot that we have to prepare your lodging. There's a room for you in the annex, but we have to straighten it up. Meanwhile, you stay here."

"I will."

Shchetinin left; the guest stood up from the sofa and began stretching, pacing, and swinging from side to side.

It was becoming cooler in the study; the evening air was wafting softly through the open windows. It was steeped in the vernal scent of birches and filled with the sounds of insects and distant echoes of diverse night sounds.

Shchetinin returned after about five minutes.

"It's not too bad: one could live here," said the guest, continuing to pace.

"I no longer even know whether it's all right or not: I've grown used to it. It must be that it really is all right."

"It is. Do you have any children?"

"What an idea! No, my friend, I don't, and thank God I don't have any yet. Before that one must prepare some things for them: one must build a nest."

"What more of a nest do you need?" asked the guest, indicating the surroundings. "Or, perhaps you plan to build each one of them a henhouse?"

"No, but in general my opinion on this question is that it's the parents' duty to prepare resources for their children, you know, their education and all that. . . . One must think about all that beforehand."

"Yes," said the guest as if pondering, continuing to pace. "Yes, that's commendable. Well then," he asked, "are the preparations proceeding well?"

"Not bad. Little by little. You can't do it all at once."

"No, you can't. Of course not. And are these . . ." asked the guest, pausing in front of Shchetinin, raising his index finger, "these reserves distributed in separate repositories: this one for Mashenka, and this one for Nikolenka? Or is it all together?"

"Come now, really!" Shchetinin cried good-humoredly. "Did you come here just to make fun of me?"

"No; I just recalled this," the guest continued, sitting down on the sofa and smiling. "My mother was a meticulous woman, very fond of her children, and a penny pincher; as soon as she gave birth to a daughter, she'd begin to put things aside for her dowry, and she had a separate chest for each of them. Well, and this was all going fairly well. The only thing was that sometimes one of them would start arguing with her; then our mother would see that things were not so good; but you couldn't get the best of her. 'Wait,' she'd say, 'you little bitch, you'll just have to do without a dowry!' Then she'd remove all the things from the unruly daughter's chest and transfer them to her obedient daughter's. What fights there were among my sisters because of this! Unbelievable fights! Only my father could make peace: he'd up and spend the dowry of all three on drink."

After this conversation both the guest and the host remained silent.

"Nevertheless, my friend, whatever you say, you can't do without it," Shchetinin said at last.

"Without what?"

"Without saving up."

"Well, each to his own. One person can't do without saving, while another can't help spending it all on drink. To each his own."

"No, wait!" Shchetinin said, interrupting him. "That's not what I mean. I understand, I do; but I'm not the sort of person you think I am."

"What sort are you? Well, tell me!"

"I'm the sort . . . I'm a man who. . . . No, I can't talk about myself. The devil only knows, I don't know how to do it."

With a worried look, Shchetinin began pacing again and tousled his hair; at last he paused, leaned his arms on the table, and said: "I can talk about what I've been doing since we last saw each other."

"Well, I don't mind. That'll be even better."

"By the way, in the beginning I wrote to you."

"What did you write? The devil knows what: some sort of appeal. You kept summoning me . . . to fulfill the duty of an honest citizen . . . about some high altar or other. . . . I threw it all in the fire right away. The hell with it, I thought, I might get in trouble. The heck with him! He's a dangerous man!"

Shchetinin roared with laughter, sprawling on the sofa.

"Ah, what an old scarecrow!" he said. "What's he talking about? Well, fine, just fine. Listen, I'll tell you all from the beginning."

"About that altar again?"

"No, no, not that. Facts! Only basic facts!"

"Fine, I like that. Go on! But wait a moment! One more question: will there be any tea? Not in the story, but here on the table? I haven't had any today. That's also an indisputable fact."

"Why, of course; yes, absolutely."

"Excellent. Now, go ahead!"

"Yes. Well," began Shchetinin after clearing his throat, "just at that time my mother passed away. Do you remember her?"

"Of course, I do. She was a venerable lady. Of course, I remember her."

"Well then, I came here after her death and got married. This woman . . . but you'll see for yourself what she's like. I can tell you one thing, if it wasn't for her, I wouldn't have been able to endure the difficult life here in the beginning, when all this was still so new and I didn't know how to do anything; there was so much unrest and no one wanted to listen: you say one thing and then another—it made no difference! Then things started to get better; we agreed to draft a land charter,[11] and all of a sudden—no! They refused: 'Let's wait.' they said, 'to see what comes next.'"

"Indeed. That's more or less a well-known story," the guest observed. "How did things end up with them?"

"How? I gave it to them."

"All of it?"

"All the land they were using."

"Was it as you expected?"

"No, by no means. It didn't turn out as I'd hoped."

---

11. An official agreement negotiated after the Emancipation in 1861 between landowners and peasants specifying the land allotments that former serfs received and the obligations they owed during the period that they remained "temporarily obligated."

"So, you didn't want to give it to them? Were you forced to, or what?"

"Not at all! I came here expecting to give it all away, and as soon as I arrived, I proposed that."

"Well, and what happened? Wouldn't they accept it?"

"Nope."

"Good for them! That's why I love the Russian people: they may not know any Latin, but they're afraid of Greeks bearing gifts."[12]

"Well, I'll be!"

"What do you mean, 'Well, I'll be'? It's perfectly understandable: if you give a man something for free, he won't take it; he thinks it's a swindle."

"Just listen to what this cost me: nights I couldn't sleep, troubles I caused, and enemies I acquired among my neighbors!"

"I'll say! Of course, you did. You set an example!"

"An example. Well then. The main thing is how they ranted and raved against it."

"Of course. You set a dreadful example."

"Such unpleasant things resulted. One fellow almost challenged me to a duel. Gossip, complaints throughout the district. . . ."

"Well, that was all for nothing. No, I would've handled it better with you. I'd simply have incited your peasants to put a bug in someone's ear."

"That happened, dear friend, everything happened."

"Well, good; it's consistent at least. What next?"

"Next? It all ended well. The mediator of the peace here[13] . . . (he's a fine fellow) became involved in the matter, explained everything to them, made sense of it all, and at last reconciled me with the peasants."

---

12. Sleptsov uses the Latin phrase "*dona ferentes*" from Virgil's *Aeneid*, II, 49: "I fear the Danaans, even those bearing gifts."

13. The office was established by statutes in 1861. The mediator was usually appointed from the local gentry landowners and his job was to assist in the implementation of the peasant reforms.

"Ah. Reconciled, you say?"

"Yes, indeed. But, take note: here's the thing! Only after three years did the peasants accept what I was offering. Now, one can ask, how much did they lose during all that time?"

"Yes, it must have been quite a bit. And, were any military officials needed to convince them to accept your gift?"

"No; thank heavens, we managed without that."

"That means they trusted the mediator alone?"

"I also explained it to them: 'Lads,' I said, 'you don't understand what's good for you.'"

"Yes, it's too bad when a person doesn't understand what's good for him. Well, no doubt, in so doing you were able to bring them down to earth?"

"What? No, my friend, that was only the beginning."

"What else was there?"

"Here's when the real problems began."

"Criminal acts?"

"Social acts, my dear friend, social."

"Yes, yes. So that's how it was!" said the guest and looked at Shchetinin with great attention. "Now I see why they informed on you; only now do I begin to understand what you wrote to me in Petersburg back then. Yes. Well, what sort of social propaganda was it?"

"You're talking nonsense; you don't understand a thing," Shchetinin replied, half joking and half serious.

"But you yourself just said it."

"What did I say? I know what you're thinking. But do you really imagine I'm capable of such schoolboy pranks?"

"I don't imagine anything. You're talking and I'm listening."

"Well then, listen carefully. I'm being serious."

"Speak!"

"I'm not engaging in anything illegal; I'm not advancing any theories; I'm doing only what each of us is obligated to do."

Shchetinin stood up from the sofa, passed his hand through his hair, and immediately sat down again: apparently he found it hard to know where to begin; he began scratching the oilcloth on the sofa. Riazanov looked him in the eye serenely and attentively.

"First of all," Shchetinin began at last, "you must agree that every social act can be lasting only if it's based on purely popular principles."

"Yes."

"As long as the common people haven't voted for it, as long as they remain silent and merely listen—then no propaganda of any sort will ever lead anywhere."

"Well, what of it?"

"Then, consequently, we must direct all our strength to ensure that . . . but perhaps you want to go to bed?"

"Yes, my friend, I do."

"We'll have plenty of time to talk about all this. What a fine host I am! The man's tired. . . . What about some tea? Wait, I'll order some now. . . ."

Shchetinin rang for a servant. Several minutes passed, but no one appeared.

"They must all have gone to bed," said Riazanov. "Never mind. Let it pass. Good night!"

"What? At least I can show you to your room. . . ."

Shchetinin hastened his step, took a candle, and led his guest to the annex.

Left alone, Riazanov got undressed, opened the window, inhaled some fresh air, looked out into the garden sunk in darkness, and became pensive. Beyond the wall someone was muttering in his sleep: "Ma-ma-mary—Maryland."[14]

Riazanov blew out the candle and went to bed.

---

14. This seems to be a reference to the American Civil War. About half the African American population in Maryland were still slaves, but the state remained faithful to the Union cause.

CHAPTER II

———

THE GUEST WOKE UP EARLY THE NEXT MORNING because next door, behind the partition, a commotion had ensued at first light: someone was walking around the room, shuffling papers, whispering, and talking to himself. Through the open window along with the morning, cool air wafted in, the cheerful sounds of bird-calls drowning out the nervous and affectionate whispering coming from the garden. The guest got dressed and sat down by the window.

"Mr. Riazanov, are you awake?" asked a familiar voice from behind the partition.

"Yes, indeed."

The clerk came in.

"My compliments to you! Well, how did you sleep? Not bad? I, God damn it, suffered all night. I heard you arrive. Once I pressed a plaster with Spanish fly[1] just behind my ear. The result? I went deaf. I went fishing and caught a cold. I went deaf."

———

1. A powder called cantharidin was derived from these brilliant green beetles and used medicinally on a plaster to raise blisters.

———

The clerk held his head a little to one side and with his hand held a plaster on his neck.

"Do you live here?" asked Riazanov.

"Yes. Just next door. This is our office. Come and see for yourself! Well? What disarray."

They entered the office; it was the same sort of room as the first: bare walls, a table with an inkwell and papers, two chairs, and a cupboard.

"Here it is, the office! Papers, books. . . . All our accounts are kept in books. We follow the Italian system of accounting with the peasant women, double entry.[2] When she has *credit* . . . ah! Her jaw drops. Such simpletons! Here's the payroll . . . a memo from the mediator of the peace. . . . Our steward's also a clever fellow. . . . 'I have the honor of humbly asking you, kind sir, to submit a declaration. . . . ' Sure they'll send it. Just wait for it! 'Coming to me at the manor house, he replied with audacity. . . . ' Hmm. What idiocy!"

The clerk rifled through some papers, read them, tossed them aside, started reading again, then suddenly tossed a packet onto the floor and said:"Why don't you sit down?"

"No, I have to go."

"As you like."

"What's over there?"

"That's where I live. It's nothing special."

He opened the door into a small room crammed with newspapers, sheet music, and trousers. . . . A dressing gown was hanging on the window; a siskin hung suspended in a cage; it was very stuffy and there was a violin lying on the bed.

"You play the violin?"

"I can't play a note. So. . . . Let's go! There's nothing else here. Where are you off to? A walk? Me too. No, I need to. Why are you standing here? Don't forget your cap."

---

2. A system of bookkeeping in which every transaction is entered as both a debit and a credit.

The courtyard was deserted. The broad shadow of the house stretched across the lawn; sparrows hopped along the brick wall.

"Where to? The garden?" asked the clerk.

"It makes no difference."

"Then let's go to the market."

"If you like. Where is it?"

"Over in the square, behind the church. It's the market square. They sell local products: tar, bast sandals . . . all sorts of other stuff! Commerce!"

A woman was walking along carrying buckets; a cook wearing a white jacket was hauling some beef up from the cellar; horses were being led to a trough for water; a setter was ambling along wagging its tail. . . .

"Tancred![3] Hey! You fool," said the clerk, petting the dog. "Now, now, now! Off you go! I've got nothing for you, not a thing. You silly dog!"

Tancred left, disgruntled.

"Ah, wait a moment," said the clerk. "I forgot something . . . a small matter. One moment."

They went into the servants' quarters.

The cook was putting some bread in the oven while an infant was crawling around beneath her feet.

"Get out of here, you little imp! What do you want?"

"Is Matvei home?" asked the clerk.

"Nope. He went off to the farm before daylight."

"Why isn't he doing something about that passport of his? He'll have to pay a fine."

"I'll tell him."

"Good. Do that. Hey, do you raise cockroaches in here?"

"Who raises them, damn them?"

"You do. You love them to death; they'll get into your ear. My goodness! What's this then? Huh? Oh, you devils! You demons

---

3. The dog is named for Tancred (1076–1112), a Norman leader in the First Crusade.

should all be torched. What? No, you're lying! You eat them, damn it. Let's go! Here, I tell you. . . ."

A peasant was making his way across the courtyard. "Greetings, Ivan Stepanych!"

"Hello! What's wrong?"

"I'm here to see you, sir."

"What for?"

"It's still about my problem."

"That heifer? I know. Did you bring the money?"

"No, I didn't."

"Well then, what is it? Did you come to chat?"

"I thought we could settle it like neighbors."

"Off with you! Bring me the money, like a neighbor!"

"Come on, Ivan Stepanych, did she really do that much damage—you must know. So she just left a lot of hoofmarks."

"We have to teach you scoundrels a lesson."

"Teach us, that's right, Ivan Stepanych; but I think we've already learned."

"No, not much."

"Well, now, let's you and I have a little talk. Your livestock wandered into my vegetable garden. . . ."

"Well, drive her away!"

"That's not hard, but why would I do it?"

"Why? The landlord will pay the fine."

"Well, that would mean bringing a suit against you! Maybe it'd be better if I didn't bother you and just broke all her legs so she wouldn't wander into my garden."

"All right. Are you done?"

"Word of honor, I'll break her legs."

"All right, my friend. It's a waste of time talking. Who needs it? What nasty folks! I tell you, they should all be whipped!"

"Really?"

"So help me, God! For pity's sake! What's going on here? They're so spoiled! So. . . . They gave 'em the land for nothing. Hey! What's the use of talking about it? There it is, the barn."

"Where?"

"Over there, the yellow one. Don't you see it?"

"What's in it?"

"Machines. Agricultural implements. . . . A waste of money. . . . No, one of them's all right. It's a curious thing—a rake. It works for a while, and then, all of a sudden, it stops working! Devil take it! Some Englishmen take money for it. No, they're clever, damn them, devil take 'em. Yes. There's this fine threshing machine. Seven hundred silver rubles for it. . . . But it makes no difference—it's all lies! It goes wherever you want it to. Those rascals! It's a funny gadget. Well, but it's too heavy, you can't do anything with it. Hey, Trofim, come over here! What are you holding?"

"A nail."

"Get going!"

They walk on a little further. The sun begins to heat up. They come to the village. Old women in blue kerchiefs are sitting with children on top of mounds piled in front of their huts; a sick calf is lying in the middle of the street warming itself; a beggar is slinking along, crying out in his rasping voice: "I'm praying for your parents, have mercy, for Christ's sake!"

The clerk paused frequently, speaking to the dogs, poking the ground with his stick, cursing, and pressing his plaster.

Some people are passing through the village wearing bast sandals, carrying scythes over their shoulders; they walk in silence, swinging their arms.

"Where are you going?" the clerk asks them.

"To the Don, to join the Cossacks," one replies.

"To mow hay, old man, hay," adds another walking past.

"Don't you have any of your own to mow?"

"We've never had any our whole life," replies a third on the run.

"Well, good luck," says the clerk.

"Thank you, my dear."

They reach the market square. A tavern stands at one end; there are awnings for traders, a shop, and a *duma*.[4] Hens are pecking in the middle of the square; quiet prevails; one can hear pigs scratching themselves on the corner of the shed, emitting low grunting sounds every so often.

The clerk and the guest enter a little shop. "Hello, Denis Ivanych," says the clerk.

"Greetings, Ivan Stepanych," replies the shopkeeper without looking up. He is sitting behind the counter in his shirtsleeves and vest, playing cards with the local clerk. The clerk is wearing a military coat and has rubber boots on his bare feet.

"Do you have any writing paper?" asks Riazanov.

"Yes. Right here. Aleksei, show him the paper! Your turn, I dealt. What do you want, Ivan Stepanych?"

"Stop playing cards! What are you doing?"

"Wait a moment! We're in the middle of a game. We've been playing for three days. What do you need? Hearts."

"Do you have any ammonium chloride?"

"What do you need it for? Go on, throw!"

"For housekeeping."

"That's my eight. You're lying. For housekeeping?"

"Yes. Do you have any?"

"Ammonium chloride?"

"Yes."

The shopkeeper looks intently at his cards and says: "Yup. So that's it. For hou-se-kee-ping. Yes, indeed. This is such a crooked game. Without the two. Ammonium chloride, eh? I don't think we have any. Well, go on, deal. Anything else?"

"Enough with your cards!"

"Well!"

"Two sticks of sealing wax."

"That we have. Aleksei, bring two sticks of office sealing wax. Ivan Stepanych, have a seat and play cards with us!"

---

4. *Author's note: Duma* is the name given in market towns to a shed where scales and weights are kept.

"To hell with you!"

"What? We're playing for nuts."

"I won't even play for nuts."

"What a miser! You even have money. How do you do!" the shopkeeper says, addressing the coachman who'd just entered.

The coachman approaches the counter silently and looks at the shelves stocked with goods.

"What it'll be?" asks the shopkeeper.

"Somewhere here, I'm looking, you used to have a kind of mirror, a round one?"

"There it is."

The coachman takes the mirror and looks at himself. The clerk rummages in the drawer with the spice cakes.

"Handsome, very handsome! There's no need to stare," the shopkeeper says good-naturedly to the coachman.

"Impossible," replies the coachman. "I want to fall in love."

"You don't say! We can see right away a man who's in a good mood. Is it the maid? Hmm. She's not bad-looking."

"She's a persuasive young woman. One word, and it's just as you like."

"I see."

"I certainly have to fall in love. Now, the main thing is, somehow or other to find a songbook."

A peasant comes into the shop. "Denis Ivanych!"

"What is it?"

"Let me go!"

"Leave the shaft bow!"

"How can I go without it? For pity's sake!"

"What do I care? There's no reason to feel sorry for you devils. Well, all right: take the shaft bow, take off your coat."

The peasant remains silent, as do all the others, and they all look at him.

"Mmm . . . here's what," the peasant mutters to himself.

Silence. The clerk cracks a nut on the counter using a weight.

"That's how it is," says the peasant, scratching the back of his head. One of his shoulders starts to sink slowly, as the coat slides off his shoulder. . . .

Pause.

"Take it off! Go on! No reason not to. It's not winter yet, my friend, you won't freeze."

The peasant sighs and moves his lips, then without a sound gradually takes off his coat, places it carefully on the counter, and leaves silently wearing only his shirt.

"Well, deal," the shopkeeper says to the clerk.

"No, I tell you," the shopkeeper says, picking up his cards.

"Yes."

"I tell you, these worthless peasants. . . . And now, how much money do you suppose I'll lose on their account? It'll vanish into thin air. Pass. I paid his poll tax."

"I'll be darned," utters the clerk with a nut in his mouth.

"That's why they're all obligated to me. Go on!"

"The heck with all of you! Goodbye!" says the clerk.

"See you soon."

After returning from the market the guest and the clerk parted. The clerk went into the office and the guest set off for the house. While crossing the courtyard he noticed several peasants, men and women, standing near the porch. A young woman in her morning housecoat stood in the doorway; she was carefully examining one peasant's finger.

"Who's that?" the guest asked the footman.

"The lady of the house."

"Hmm."

The guest drew near the porch. The woman standing in the doorway was a bit taken aback, but immediately recovered and returned to the peasant's finger with even greater attention.

"Wait a moment, I'll give you a break," she said, suddenly glancing over at the guest: he was standing directly opposite, staring straight into her face. He bowed; she said "Hello" quietly and continued talking with the peasant in a determined manner: "Perhaps you have a splinter?"

"Who knows? No, take a look, I doubt it."

"Put some of this on a little rag and place it on your finger, and then come back in a day or two."

"Back 'ere, to see you?"

"Yes, yes, back here!"

"All right, I will."

"And what's wrong with you?"

On the threshold stood a stout but pale-looking peasant, breathing heavily.

"What's wrong with you?"

"It's not good, ma'am. Been a long time."

"In what way? Do you feel feverish?"

"No, I don't. And I haven't been sweating."

"Are you eating?"

"Not at all! For a week I couldn't even eat a little bowl of kasha. Just see how my belly's all swollen up. You could crush lice on it."

The guest looked at the mistress of the house: one muscle in her face twitched slightly; then she regained her composure and said hurriedly: "You've probably caught cold."

"I don't know, ma'am, whether I did or not. If I didn't, then this illness must've been brought on by the wind. I woke up in the morning and looked down at my feet: swollen, like two blocks. Then I started to swell and swell, and it got worse and worse. . . ."

"'Looked down at his feet,'" muttered the guest in a low voice. "Up to now he didn't even know he had feet."

The mistress glanced at the guest, first in earnest, then she smiled hesitantly, and once again assumed a serious expression.

The guest stood there a while longer and then went into the house. He found Shchetinin in his study sitting at the window with a newspaper.

"I stopped by to see you," said Shchetinin, "but they told me you'd gone off somewhere."

"I went for a walk," said the guest, sitting down on the sofa. "Do you get up early?"

"I got up around five this morning and went out to check on the work."

"So, you take a serious interest in the management of your estate?"

"Indeed, I do! It's nothing to make light of, my friend."

"Yes," said Riazanov, as if reflecting; then he added, "There's this kind of animal—a beaver, a river animal, a sturdy beast; he moves slowly, as if he's always thinking about something; he has a rich coat, beaver fur, and his face is just like a contractor's. And what sort of passion inspires this beast? Building things. That's why he's called a beaver-builder, *Castor fiber*.[5] Wherever you relocate him, even to a bell tower, if you provide him with some brushwood, he'll immediately start building a dam. He'd even say about himself that he couldn't possibly do without it."

"Well, yes. What can I say: you make fun of everything. Let's go, my friend, and have some tea. Here's the mistress of the house."

The sounds of a woman's rustling dress and of rattling crockery could be heard in the dining room. The guest and his host went in.

"Here, let me introduce you," said Shchetinin to his wife, "my friend and persecutor, Iakov Vasil'ich Riazanov. Please get to know each other."

The mistress paused for a moment; holding the teapot in one hand, she extended her other hand to the guest. "We've already seen each other," she said to her husband.

"When was that?"

"I just came upon Mar'ia Nikolavna," said the guest, "out on the porch, healing the infirm."

Mar'ia Nikolavna smiled slightly, but immediately knit her brow and regained control of her face.

"Do you find that amusing?" she asked, pouring the tea and blushing a bit.

"No, not amusing."

---

5. The Latin name of the Eurasian species of beaver.

"Tell me, please," said Shchetinin, placing his hands on the table, "what is it in Petersburg that everyone's so involved in that you can't talk about anything seriously?"

"No, not everyone," Riazanov replied earnestly and began stirring his tea.

After a brief silence, he repeated, as if to himself, "Not everyone." Staring into his glass, he continued: "No, there are some people who talk about everything seriously. There are even more of that kind. Once I met one on the street when I was going to the bathhouse. 'It's time,' he said, 'for us really to get down to business.' I said, 'Yes,' I said, 'it's time, really,' I said, 'it's time. Goodbye.' 'Where are you off to?' he asks. 'I'm going to the bathhouse,' I said, 'to have a bath.' 'Yes,' he says, 'you're always making fun. I'm being serious.' Well, what's to be done?" Riazanov suddenly asked, raising his head. "I had also answered him seriously, yet he thought I was making fun."

"What are you saying . . . " Shchetinin started to say, but Riazanov continued: "No, it depends on the person. One talks seriously, but always seems to be making fun; take Suvorov, for instance; he crowed like a rooster; however, everyone understood that he was about to play a dirty trick."[6]

Mar'ia Nikolavna looked closely at the guest from behind the samovar.

"No, really," Shchetinin began, "I've been noticing that Petersburg has the tendency to break one of the habits of regarding things directly; one's sense of reality completely disappears; one seems not to notice it; it just doesn't exist."

"You're talking about redemption payments, aren't you?"[7] asked Riazanov.

---

6. Alexander Suvorov (1720–1800) was a Russian military commander notable for his achievements in the Russo-Turkish War of 1787–1791 and in the French Revolutionary Wars. He often joked with his men and shrewdly presented the results of detailed planning and careful strategy as the work of inspiration.

7. After the Emancipation Russian serfs were required to pay landowners for their allocation of land in a series of redemption payments.

"No, my friend, I'm talking about something else. I'm talking about the crude reality that surrounds us and makes itself felt at every step."

"Well, God only knows," replied Riazanov, "who feels it more. It seems to everyone that he does."

"Stay here a while, my friend, and observe us, unskilled laborers, how we cope with the raw material here; perhaps it'll alter your view. That's what, my friend," Shchetinin added, slapping his guest on the knee.

"Perhaps," Riazanov replied with a smile.

"What are you laughing at? Just look, I'll show you what these people I have to deal with are really like."

"Yes, indeed."

"Then you'll see for yourself what we have to do: not only do we have to help them but we also have to persuade and entreat them so they'll permit us to be of use to them."

"Yes. It's just as Hamlet says; 'Virtue itself of vice must pardon beg, / Yea, curb and woo for leave to do him good.'"[8]

"Yes, my friend, 'vice must beg pardon.' . . . I'm being serious. If you've taken on the job, you're in no mood for irony."

"What sort of irony? That's more philanthropy, not irony."

"Well, I don't know what it's called, but I do know that one of our lesser brothers is on his way over here to see me now,"[9] Shchetinin said, looking out the window. "And I also know he'll ask me to give him back his heifer, but I won't do it."

"Why not?" asked Mar'ia Nikolavna.

"Because that's the way it should be."

Shchetinin quickly drained his glass of tea and went into the vestibule. The door from the dining room had remained open.

"Hello! What do you want?" he asked the peasant just then coming in from the hall.

---

8. *Hamlet*, Act III, sc. iv, lines 151–52.

9. An expression borrowed from Matthew 25:40, "Inasmuch as ye have done it unto one of the least of these my brethren, ye have done it unto me."

The peasant bowed. "Coming to see you, your honor."

"What for?"

"Still about the same thing. Master, Leksan Vasil'ich!"[10] The peasant sank to his knees.

"You're still pestering me about that heifer? Get up, man, get up! Aren't you ashamed? How many times have I said it's offensive. I won't even talk to you unless you stand up."

The peasant got up.

"Well, listen here! You must understand that I don't need your money; it won't make me rich. I'm fining you for your own good, so that in future you'll be more careful and won't let your livestock get out of hand. You'll even thank me for teaching you some good sense."

"I'm very content, master, Leksan Vasil'ich. I humbly thank you."

"Well, you see! Do you understand now that it's for your own good?"

"I understand, sir."

"Well, if you do, there's nothing more to talk about. I'll show you that I won't ask one extra kopeck from you. Here's the list, all right? It's a printed list from the minister about how much to collect for damages. It says here that for a cow, from the 1st of June through the 1st of July—it's one ruble and fifty kopecks. . . ."

"Yes, sir."

"And sustenance for three days—twenty kopecks a day, so that's sixty kopecks more. The total comes to two rubles and ten kopecks. Right?"

"Exactly."

"We could check it on the abacus."

"No, there's no need."

"Well, so what else do you want from me?"

"Nothing. . . . And now about, that's to say . . . we doubt even more, that it's like neighbors . . .

---

10. The peasant employs a shortened, colloquial version of Shchetinin's name.

"Not like neighbors! I told you already."

"Yes, sir, you did."

"It's the law. Do you understand? The law."

"Yes, sir."

"So what can I do? Huh?"

The peasant was silent. From the dining room, Riazanov, his beard resting on the back of a chair, was watching this scene; Mar'ia Nikolavna was forming little balls out of a piece of bread.

"Order me to pray to God for you forever," the peasant said suddenly, dropping to his knees again.

Shchetinin spat in disgust and walked out. The peasant remained there on his knees for several minutes, looked around, looked around again, sighed, and then got up and walked across the courtyard, one step at a time, holding his cap in his two hands.

"Well, what do you think? How do you find this lesser brother?"

Mar'ia Nikolavna locked the sugar bowl away and went into the next room. Shchetinin paced the dining room and opened the window.

"God knows, it's stuffy in here! These lesser brethren are swine, that's all I can tell you."

"No, I see that you don't know how to beg pardon of vice so that it'd let you . . . impose a fine on yourself," said Riazanov, sitting at the table.

"What a good-for-nothing that peasant is!" Shchetinin continued in the meantime. "When he needs something from me, he comes, begs, and kisses my feet, but if I need to buy a dozen eggs from him, he's ready to clean me out."

"That's sensible. Well, what about the others? Are they any better?"

"To tell the truth, the others also have their ups and downs; but that's not the point. We're the ones to blame. We must instill greater trust in them; we need to be stricter with ourselves, and then they'll also. . . ."

"Charge less for their eggs? Probably."

"No, they'll be stricter with themselves."

"Will they?"

"Of course, they will."

"What for?"

"They'll see for themselves."

"What?"

"That it's better that way."

"Do you yourself really believe it'll be better?"

"I'll say! Why are you looking at me like that? What sort of worker would I be if I didn't believe in the success of the task I was undertaking?"

"That is—certitude of things invisible, as if they were visible,[11] in that which is desired and anticipated, as if it were real. Yes, that's nice."

Shchetinin, without replying, stood at the window pensively regarding the courtyard; then, coming to his senses, he added: "Yes! There's the building site—I must visit it. Masha!"

Mar'ia Nikolavna came into the dining room; Riazanov went out onto the balcony.

"I'm heading out," Shchetinin said to his wife. "A peasant woman will be coming here to see me. Please talk to her!"

"About what?"

"She'll tell you all about it herself. Well, you'll see."

"All right."

"Have a good talk with her. You know, how you can have a *good* talk."

Mar'ia Nikolavna smiled. "Do I ever have talks that aren't good?"

"No; never, never. You're so clever! Well, give me a kiss!"

The open carriage was brought up to the porch.

Riazanov stood on the balcony and looked into the garden.

---

11. Ironic reference to the beginning of the Nicene Creed: "I believe in one God, the Father Almighty, Maker of heaven and earth, and of all things visible and invisible."

Directly opposite him through the green grove of acacias one could see the old summerhouse with its dilapidated roof, overgrown with burdock and nettles; apple trees were blooming in the distance. A white bell tower stood beyond the garden, and then it was all meadows, ponds glistening in the sun, green hills, and more meadows. It was getting warm in the garden; from time to time soft streams of fragrant freshness drifted through the air, together with the hurried twittering of robins hiding beneath the bushes. Riazanov stood for a while on the balcony and then went to stroll in the garden. In one lane he happened upon an old gardener wearing a white shirt, sporting a white beard, carrying a head of lettuce beneath one arm. The gardener doffed his cap and bowed low. A child's suntanned face with a pod in his mouth flashed in the bushes, but he vanished as soon as Riazanov glanced at him; from behind came a chirping sound—and five children jumped into the raspberry canes as fast as their legs could carry them. Lagging behind all of them a little girl ran crying, shouting as loud as she could, "Ma-a-a." A house servant was doing the laundry in the pond. After noticing Riazanov, she tucked up her skirt, and without turning around, bowed to him from the rear. The ducks hiding along the shore noisily set out onto the water. . . .

Riazanov was about to return to his room in the annex, but just as he was walking past the house, he suddenly heard the sound of someone crying in the hall. He went onto the porch. Mar'ia Nikolavna stood in the vestibule talking with a peasant woman. The woman was weeping, and Mar'ia Nikolavna also looked distraught; trying to conceal her embarrassment, she said to Riazanov: "Just listen to what she's saying."

Riazanov remained standing there, and the peasant woman, paying him no attention, continued whimpering, and said: "I sez to 'im: you sho' be 'shamed. . . ."

"And what did he do?" asked Mar'ia Nikolavna.

"He sez: me be 'shamed? I'll pull out ya' braid first, he sez, then I'll be 'shamed."

"Hmm," said Riazanov.

"Yes, that's what, ma'am," continued the peasant woman, blow-ing her nose in her sleeve, "wha' can I say? Wha' can we do but be sad over our children, but wha' of it? He's got only mischief in mind, tryin' to be clever at our sister's expense. They're such wise guys!"

"I still don't understand why he beats you," said Mar'ia Nikolavna.

"Why?" the peasant woman repeated. "Ya' think a peasant should have reasons. He don't say why. He thinks a woman ain't worth a thing. She turns up—bang. Go away, he sez, get away from me, ya' hag!" The peasant woman wiped away her tears with the hem of her apron. "What the devil good, he sez, are ya' to me, huh? I never seen anything so weak. You, he sez, only thing ya' good for is scarin' crows."

"He doesn't love you," Mar'ia Nikolavna commented softly.

"What? Doesn't love me? What am I to 'im? I'm not a stranger. Love! Why should he love me? My chest feels all stuffed up; I can't do anythin', nothin' at all. Ya' think I'm glad to be so heavy?"

"Yes, indeed! So that's it," said Riazanov and went back to his room in the annex.

Shchetinin returned from the village before dinner, weary and covered with dust; he took off his tie, drank a glass of vodka, and sat down at the table in silence.

"Well, how's the construction work going?" Mar'ia Nikolavna asked him.

"It's going," he replied reluctantly. "I'm dog-tired." He fell silent for a while and placed his spoon down on the table. "Those carpenters are such swine! They made it so now we have to raise the lower beams. They didn't number them as they were supposed to and got mixed up. The result's such a mess that it's awful to look at: one beam goes one way, another goes the other. I'd selected the best lumber, but they spoiled it all. Now, don't you see, we'll have a lot of work to reset the frame all over again! Damn them! I cursed and abused them. . . . What scoundrels! Ah, I forgot you were here."

"Never mind, don't be embarrassed," replied Riazanov, continuing to eat.

"No, they really try my patience."

"Well, of course," remarked Riazanov.

"Judge for yourself," Shchetinin continued. "I pay them almost twice as much as they'd receive elsewhere; then, besides that, I feed them and I pay their salary by the month."

"Yes."

"They came to see me, all ragged, and fell on their knees before me: 'Dear father, we've nothing to eat, give us work!' Well, I felt sorry for them, took them on, clothed them, gave them shoes, paid the poll tax for two of them,[12] and gave each one a ruble in advance. . . ."

"And such ingratitude!"

"No, so what? You really try. Well, didn't I try as hard as I could? So this is the trick they played on me. They don't even want to hear that I took a loss of fifty rubles on their account. The beams were too far away, don't you see, and they were too lazy to bring them. Huh? How do you like that?"

"Not much. It's dishonest on their part," said Riazanov, wiping his mouth with his napkin.

"No, seriously?"

"What of it? It's clear that you can't approve such performance."

"Well, you see. Now you tell me, did I have the right to call them swindlers?"

"No; you have no right to call them swindlers."

"Why not?"

"Because by law you're not allowed to. You might want to do all sorts of things. You can't. Haven't they been freed from serfdom?"

"Yes."

"Well, so? You just can't do it. It's a personal insult. But as for turning to the district police officer—that's another matter."

"But I don't want that."

"If not, then it's best to take your complaint directly to the mediator of the peace, so a ruling would be made on some basis,

12. The major direct tax introduced by Peter I in 1724 and levied on the entire male population of the taxpaying strata; that is, all categories of peasants, guild merchants, and artisans.

and so on. That's much more reliable and . . . more respectable than abusing them."

"Oh, but no. You don't. . . ."

"You think they won't follow up? No, my friend, times are different now. They'll call them to account for the last kopeck."

"You don't say!"

"They won't get to wriggle out of it, don't worry."

All this while Mar'ia Nikolavna followed the conversation with rapt attention, glancing uneasily first at Riazanov, then at her husband; at last she couldn't hold back any longer. Blushing, she asked in an agitated voice: "But is it a good thing to go to court?"

"Do you think it's a bad thing? Why?" Riazanov asked her amiably.

"Because . . . they'll punish them. . . . I don't know. . . ."

"Well, so what?"

"What—what do you mean, so what? They'll throw them in jail. . . . On the whole that's. . . ."

"Perhaps they'll send them to jail. If exhortations don't work and gentle measures won't win them over. . . ."

"But they're poor. You forget that. . . . Where will they get fifty rubles?"

"If they don't have it in cash, they can use their personal property or livestock."

"Well, and. . . ."

"They'll sell something, ma'am. That's their own business."

"Why, I don't even know what to call that . . . it's brutality!"

"Very possibly, ma'am."

"So you propose to employ such measures?"

"I don't propose any measures; I merely want to remind him."

"Of what?"

"His obligations. Every right imposes on a person certain obligations. If you enjoy the right—then fulfill the obligations."

"What obligations? You remind him that, if he wishes, he can abuse his right."

"Not at all, ma'am. On the contrary: I remind him only how to acquire it; he's the one who abuses it."

"Is it really abuse, if he forgives these carpenters?"

"What did you think? Of course, it's abuse. If he exercised only his right to punish and pardon, so be it; let him do what he wants. If God gave him such a kind soul, what's there to talk about? If you want to go begging, be my guest. But don't forget there are lots of us, and that he, by leaving these builders unpunished, is encouraging them to try more swindles and he's setting a bad example. And we all suffer as a result: he's ruining our workers."

Shchetinin stared at his plate thoughtfully and moved his fork over it.

"Well, it's a good thing," continued Riazanov, "that I can live here doing nothing; but if I were a worker, I'd . . . I'd be ruined immediately. I'd say: 'Ah! So that's it! I can do anything I want. Go off to a tavern—hey, fellows, you workers, let's go off and find work! Let's go find work planting a garden; we'll get paid in advance, and then we'll plant all the trees upside down, dig up all the paths, and leave. Just you try to find us!' Well, would that be all right?"

"God knows," Shchetinin said at last, "why you're saying all this."

"I'm saying it because I don't want to deprive you of any friendly advice. I see that my friend's hesitating, feeling threatened that he may fall victim to his own weakness, and play dirty tricks on everyone; well, I can't refrain from reminding him. I say, 'My friend, be careful, don't yield to temptation, don't commit unlawful indulgences, because it'll encroach on our property in some insolent manner. A sacred right's been profaned; the fatherland's in danger. . . . Take courage, my friend,' I say, 'and hasten to hand those workers who've deceived you over into the hands of justice. . . .'"

Shchetinin started laughing; Mar'ia Nikolavna smiled hesitantly, and the footman, standing at a distance holding a clean plate in his hand and knitting his brows, glanced up sullenly first at one, then at the other; obviously he couldn't understand a thing.

"You say 'hand them over,'" began Shchetinin. "Well, all right: what would you say if I actually did that?"

"What would I say? I'd say: here's a model landowner! And I'd be proud of your friendship. I'd say: he's a consistent fellow; and who could utter higher praise for you?"

"So that's the way it is," Shchetinin said with a sigh. "But, no, my friend, I think that in certain circumstances one must act inconsistently. Masha, pour me some kvass!"[13]

"Yes. Well, as you like. It goes without saying. I won't force you; it's only that. . . ."

"But don't you see," Shchetinin interrupted him. "The thing is that such strict consistency is impossible in practical affairs. It can't be required."

"Well, yes. It can't be required of us, but it can from the builders. That's true."

"No, it's not. They can't be compared."

"Why not?"

"First of all because they have no definite goal toward which they're striving."

"I see! I'm eager to know on what basis you arrived at that conclusion."

"From what I observe every day."

"For example?"

"They try to work only as little as possible and receive as much as possible."

"Hmm. Well, in my opinion, that's a rather definite goal. What else do you have? You said they have no goal."

"Is that really a goal?"

"So what is it?"

"The devil only knows what it is, some unconscious aspiration."

"Aspiration! An aspiration usually posits some goal. Well, all right, let's suppose it's an aspiration, even an unconscious one.

---

13. A fermented beverage made from black or regular rye bread.

What are they aspiring for? As you say, to work as little as possible and receive as much as possible. You consider that this aspiration isn't good. Well, now let me ask you, what are you striving for? To work as much as possible and receive as little as possible? Is that it?"

"N-no. . . ."

"Well, what else is there to say? Consequently, we share the same aspirations; the only difference is that we desire consciously to apply them to our estates, while they, like all dim-witted folk, unconsciously balk and try to scheme in all possible ways. Well, in that case we have the means to compel them, instruments adapted to the ways of the common people. In ancient times customs were crude—then even the tools required by the dim-witted for their work were also somehow unimproved: police superintendents, district police officers, and so on; now, when customs are significantly gentler, country folk have fully recognized the necessity of enlightenment, and laxer, more spiritual measures of compulsion, so to speak, are employed, namely: admonitions, fines, remote granaries, and so forth. And we busy ourselves in this manner, and will continue to do so, until a measure of our lawless acts is fulfilled. But why stand on ceremony, why keep sniveling, that I don't understand. It's all very simple; the whole question is 'who wins';[14] of course, the main thing is not to be shy. . . ."

"Clear the table," Shchetinin said to the footman as he stood up from behind the table.

14. Literally, "Who, whom?," a Russian saying found in works by Gogol, Turgenev, and others that was later adopted by Lenin as the fundamental question of politics: "Who will dominate whom?"

CHAPTER III

————

AROUND EIGHT O'CLOCK IN THE EVENING, TWO DAYS after his arrival, Riazanov took a stroll along the riverbank. The sandy path on which he walked wound among bushes and led to a mill. A stony precipice rose steeply on the other side; it was covered with reddish hazelnut trees, mixed in with low curly oak. From the sloping bank one could see a gray, pitted road winding bravely into the mountains, the green roof of a watermill, and the manor house itself half enveloped in greenery. The sun was no longer visible, but the steep bank of the river was bathed entirely in reddish light. There was a strong smell of dampness and reeds from the bushes. Riazanov walked slowly, his feet sinking deep into the cold sand. When he heard the sound of wheels behind him, he turned to look: a horse's head with a yoke was moving through the bushes; he saw a boy in a large cap and a priest wearing a green cassock and a hat with a wide brim. The priest was riding on a cart; when it caught up with Riazanov, the priest inquired: "I see you've gone fishing again? Oh, I beg your pardon! I was mistaken. I thought you were the office clerk," said the priest, taking off his hat.

————

"My compliments to you," said Riazanov.

"Good evening. By any chance are you going to Mr. Shchetinin's? Please take a seat. To tell you the truth, I was also about to visit him."

Riazanov got into the cart. Off they went.

"You're probably a visitor? Well, yes. I kept looking to see who it was. I was wrong. Ha, ha, ha! Splendid! Are you from Saratov?"[1]

"No, from Petersburg."

"Ah. A resident of the capital. You've decided to visit our region?"

"Yes, indeed."

'Hmm. Splendid. Your name?"

"Iakov."

"Yes, yes, Iakov, our Lord's brother.[2] Your patronymic?"

"Vasil'ich."

"Iakov Vasil'ich. Yes. Well, Iakov Vasil'ich, and do you own your own home in Petersburg?"

"No, I don't."

"Hmm. You rent an apartment?"

"I do."

"Are you a civil servant?"

"No, I'm not."

"No. Didn't want to be one?"

"No."

"Well, of course, it's not for everyone. Do you have your own assets?"

"No, I don't."

"Are you of noble rank?"

"Ecclesiastical."

"Really!" The priest turned to look at him. "Well, then. I'm very glad. Let's get acquainted."

They reached the dam. Near the mill stood some horses and several peasants dusted with flour; water rumbled softly in the

---

1. A major city, the administrative center of Saratov Oblast, and an important port on the Volga River.

2. Iakov is the Russian equivalent of James.

wheels, ducks swam around on the pond; the cart bounced over some hummocks. It was growing dark; Riazanov sat next to the priest; the wind blew the hair of the priest's beard and during their conversation strands kept winding up in Riazanov's mouth. Meanwhile the priest asked: "Did you earn a first-class degree? Why weren't you ordained as a priest? Couldn't you find a wife?[3] Ah! Yes; you didn't want to be one."

The cart arrived at the courtyard of the manor house; peasants were crowding around the porch where Shchetinin stood, notebook in hand; he was speaking, pointing a pencil at one fellow's nose: "If I were to sell you even one more withy[4] like that, you can spit in my face."

"Well, Leksan Vasil'ich!" the peasants began.

"No, my dears; I've had quite enough; you've got enough already. Ah, hello, father!"

"My compliments to you," said the priest, tucking up his cassock and climbing onto the porch. "In the name of the Father, the Son, and the Holy. . . . What's going on here? Are they trying to deceive you again?"

"Nothing new in that!" Shchetinin made a dismissive gesture.

"Tell me, please! Are they from Kriukov?[5] You're from Kriukov, right?"

"We are," the peasants replied unwillingly.

"Well, then. I know them very well. Indeed. I can assure you, they're regular rascals."

The peasants looked coldly at the priest; one coughed into his cap.

"Why are you coughing?" the priest asked suddenly. "You can't hide from me, my dear fellow. Please," he continued, turning to Shchetinin, "with this same peasant. . . . What's your name? Semën, isn't it?"

---

3. According to church regulations, a man who completes seminary could be ordained only after he was married.

4. A tough, flexible twig used for binding.

5. A town in southeastern Ukraine.

"Yes."

"Yes, well it was with this same Semën that last year I decided to share in keeping some bees. He talked me into it, the scoundrel. He agreed. 'And I agree,' I said. Come here, you! Why are you hiding? Well, all right. I said, 'Now look here, Semën.' He said, 'Don't you worry!' Fine. To tell the truth, I was counting on him. And, just think, he cheated me! That is, he did it so slyly, you couldn't even imagine it better. This very same measly peasant. He's such a hypocrite. . . . I want to lodge a complaint against him with the mediator."

"I beg your pardon, father," the peasant started to speak.

"Don't lie! I know you're a liar. What of it? You deceived me to my face, right to my face. And, in so doing, my good man, you really insulted me: you deceived your spiritual father. Huh? I hope you're happy."

"Come have some tea," said Mar'ia Nikolavna, coming out on the porch.

Everyone gathered in the dining room around the samovar: Mar'ia Nikolavna buttered some bread, Shchetinin was about to sit down at the table, but instead got up again, picked up his notebook, and began writing; Riazanov drummed his fingers on the table; the priest stared at the candlestick in silence.

"Did you pay a lot for this?" he asked Mar'ia Nikolavna at last.

"I don't know. He's the one who bought it."

"What?" Shchetinin asked, glancing into his notebook.

"The father's asking about the candlesticks."

"Are they expensive?" the priest repeated.

"About five rubles, I think," Shchetinin replied rapidly.

"Nice piece of work," observed the priest, putting one down.

"Two rubles eight grivnas,[6] plus one ruble seventy-two, plus fifty kopecks," Shchetinin muttered under his breath.

"The price of hay these days is so high," said the priest, after a little pause; not eliciting any sympathy from the others, he turned

---

6. A grivna was originally a unit of currency in medieval Russia, and at this time was worth ten kopecks.

to Riazanov: "And where you live, Iakov Vasil'ich, I suppose there's also hay. . . . By any chance, do you sometimes purchase any?"

"What would I need it for?"

"So, you don't keep horses?"

"No, I don't."

"Yes, I see. But, you buy flour, don't you? How much does that cost?"

"God knows. I don't get involved."

Mar'ia Nikolavna smiled.

"Why are you discussing such things with him, father?" Shchetinin began, stashing the notebook in his pocket. "Why, he's . . . you think he knows anything? He makes fun of everything."

The priest threw an uneasy glance at Riazanov.

"But I only . . . I didn't ask anything like that . . . usually. . . . What's there to laugh at? Go on, laugh."

"You don't know him."

"No, I don't. I didn't say anything bad. If I'd asked something indecent . . . but I spoke in your wife's presence. . . . Mar'ia Niko-lavna heard it. I even asked rather discreetly: 'How much does flour cost in St. Petersburg?'"

"Why do you want to provoke a quarrel between me and the priest?" asked Riazanov. "We just met, and you're trying to set him against me. That's not good."

Mar'ia Nikolavna hastened to change the subject and began hurriedly: "Father, a countrywoman came to see me today."

"Yes."

"She's complaining that her husband doesn't love her."

"Tsk!"

The priest looked concerned.

"Yes, she's an unfortunate woman," said Shchetinin.

"You don't say!"

"I've been wanting to talk to you about it for some time. She keeps coming to see me; judge for yourself, what can I do about it?"

"Well, of course. Wouldn't it be better if she went directly to see the mediator?"

"I agree with you," observed Riazanov. "The mediator. That's his explicit responsibility."

"Naturally," the priest affirmed.

"No. Don't you see, father," Shchetinin continued, not listening to the others. "I think you could put in a word of warning to produce some effect. . . ."

"How?"

"That is, on the woman's husband."

"Yes; a word of warning. . . . Well then? All right. If that's what you want. It's possible."

"Try it, really."

"With pleasure. Of course, you know, this rudeness of theirs, well, on the other hand. . . ."

"You and your humaneness," said Riazanov to Shchetinin. "You will make it the priest's responsibility."

The priest glanced uneasily first at Riazanov, then at Shchetinin.

"The father's a spiritual healer, and this, my friend, is a criminal matter."

"How so?"

"Why, it's very simple: the peasant, don't you see, is beating his wife, and he's doing so because she's expecting; it's clear what could happen."

"Hmm. What a shame," said the priest after a moment's thought.

"Exactly," Riazanov agreed.

"No, the devil only knows what's going on here!" said Shchetinin, tossing his spoon onto the table. "So then, in your opinion, should he be allowed to beat this woman as much as he wants?"

"I'm eager to know how you could prevent it."

"Very simply. . . ."

"I see! Please tell us. The priest and I are listening."

"It's no big deal! Take her away from him, and that's that."

"What do you think of that?" Riazanov asked the priest.

"No, Aleksandr Vasil'ich, that's really too . . ." said the priest with a laugh, slapping Shchetinin amiably on the knee. "That's a little . . . it's not right. No, not right. . . . And now, Aleksandr

Vasil'ich," he said, standing up from behind the table, "I'd like to trouble you about a small matter."

"What's that?"

"About the hay."

After tea Mar'ia Nikolavna went into the hall and began playing some variations on the piano; Riazanov, slipping his hands into his pockets, stood on the terrace; Shchetinin, deep in thought, walked up and down the hall with the priest; a lamp was burning in the living room. Spreading his arms wide, the priest said: "There's nothing to be done. If only they understood something; so help me God, it just makes you want to laugh and cry at the same time. You just used the word 'conviction.' Yes. Once I was sitting in class and asked a peasant lad (I must say, he was no longer so young), 'Who,' I say, 'created the world?' And he replies, 'The village elder,' he says. There you are!"

Shchetinin made no reply.

"No, I always remember Mr. Shishkin," continued the priest. "I must say he was a smart landowner and had such zeal for the church, it was a wonder."

"Hmm," Shchetinin muttered absentmindedly.

"Now, it used to be that all of his peasants would attend vespers. If any of them dawdled—they'd have to work on a holiday without pay![7] And what do you think, if you don't remind them, they'd even forget to cross themselves in church. Real cretins."

Mar'ia Nikolavna closed the lid of the piano, approached the men, and asked: "Father, how do you like that waltz?"

"A splendid piece," he replied.

After a little pause, all three of them went out onto the terrace.

It was a warm spring night in the garden with pale blue stars shining in the fading sky. Through the delicate fog one could see barely visible shadows of birches and sandy paths winding among them. A sort of impenetrable quiet drew nearer and nearer, envel-

---

7. The *barshchina*, or corvée, was the system of forced, unpaid labor of peasants on the landlord's estate during the time of serfdom.

oping bushes and trees, and swallowing the restless swishing and timid rustling of the branches.

The four people who'd just come onto the terrace paused in silence before the dark garden and, as if encased by this dark quiet, stood listening to something for quite a while.

"My goodness," said the priest with a sigh at last; looking up at the sky, he added, "What mystery!"

"What did you say, father?" asked Mar'ia Nikolavna.

"'What mystery,' I say."

"Yes. But I thought. . . ."

"No, sir. And what does Mr. Riazanov have to say?" said the priest. "Where are you? I can't see you. Ah, here," continued the priest, finding Riazanov. "You're so forthright with your words. . . ."

"Well, so what?"

"No, I've noticed that your heart's embittered. Do you recall what's written about those who're so headstrong?[8] There's something to that. You certainly know how to make fun of things, but you don't know what's good. Consequently, you've forgotten what you were taught."

"How can one remember everything? We were taught all sorts of things."

"Better to wait before you make fun; first you ought to have another look at the Good Book."

"I'd be glad to review it," said Riazanov, climbing the stairs onto the terrace, "but I never have time."

"Shall we have something to eat, ladies and gentlemen?" Shchetinin asked suddenly.

---

8. A reference to Jeremiah 19:9: "And I will cause them to eat the flesh of their sons and the flesh of their daughters, and they shall eat every one the flesh of his friend. . . ."

CHAPTER IV

———

A WEEK PASSED. NO FUNDAMENTAL CHANGE OCCURRED either in their activities or in the Shchetinins' way of life. Riazanov was hardly ever seen or heard in the house: in the early morning he went off into the fields, or he clambered along the hilly riverbank and sat under a tree reading a book until dinner; or else he went off with the clerk's son to one of the little islands, where he sat on the pebbles for hours, watching the lad fish; sometimes he would drop by the shop. After dinner many folks would gather there to sit and chat: the district clerk, house serfs, and sometimes, someone traveling along the road would call in to have a smoke and a drink. Three people would be sitting there playing cards. Riazanov would sit near the entrance to the shop, looking out at the street. The heat was oppressive; cured sturgeon was hanging over the door dripping fat and flies were swarming all around it; in the shop verbal abuse was being traded over the game of cards: "Now I'll allow myself five hits," cries the shopkeeper.

"What right do you have to peek at the cards?" asks the clerk. "I didn't."

———

"Yes, you did."

"I want to be a rascal."

"That's what you are."

"Come on, then," says the peasant passing through and holding out his glass. The young boy pours him some vodka. The peasant crosses himself and prepares to drink. A fly suddenly lands in his glass.

"Damn it all," says the peasant, fishing out the fly. "Well, my friend, I crossed myself for nothing."

"That's a sign of good luck, that fly is," says the boy.

"That's right, friend, good luck. It's the luck of a peasant—a fly. Ah, but your vodka's good and strong," says the peasant, hacking and spitting.

Returning home in the evening, Riazanov would usually find a group of peasant women and girls in the office; the clerk was settling accounts for work completed and was always angry, arguing and swearing. Through the partition he could hear the women whispering, snorting, and pushing each other; Ivan Stepanych (the clerk) was shouting at them: "Hey, you clowns! Did you come here to play games?"

"You hear?" they said, trying to quiet one another.

"Were there many of you weeding your land? What are you here for? You've already been told. Hey, you, what's your name? Aniutka! Where's your notebook? You vile creature, you messed it up. Look here! Who dug those rows? Was it you, huh?"

"Ivan Stepanych!"

"Well?"

"Look at my notebook."

"I'll show you! Where's your husband?"

"He's a soldier now."

"What's there to look at?"

"And what's this?"

"This? It's called 'carrying forward.' Understand? You fool! You don't know anything. Go over there and stand by the stove."

"Ivan Stepanych, there's somethun' I want to ask ya.'"

"Go on!"

"What if I give birth to a boy, what's he. . . ."

"Get out!"

After finishing the accounting with the peasant women, Ivan Stepanych would sometimes stop by to see Riazanov and share with him the latest political news, like, for instance: "Have you read the newspapers? General Grant's received reinforcements. It also says that General Meade's crossed the Rapidan River and reached General Lee's main forces.[1] He'll move again quickly. Ah, damn it! But they've a long way to catch up to Major Zankisov."[2]

"Yes, of course," Riazanov confirmed.

"It says in the *Moscow News*: all in white, sitting on a white horse, he races ahead, sporting a white badge. He swoops down—just like that! Some women sent him a letter from Petersburg: 'Kuzma Ivanych, do us a favor, we've heard this and that, all about your valorous deeds . . . we're full of astonishment and gratitude . . . sporting a badge amid the dangers of battle. . . . Be so kind, they say, here's our work . . . from women devoted to you.'"

"Aha. That's good," said Riazanov.

"No, listen to this: this Polish *rząd*[3] is all theirs—damn it! And these *gminy*[4] are the devil knows what. They say: now, they say, we've seen the light. Huh? No, they're clever, damn them. Yes. And in the village of Grabli a peasant named Leon, age twenty, puts on a sheepskin coat with the wool to the outside, and sets off one evening to the house of one Semën Mazur, but this one, 'Bang!' and shoots him with a rifle. That's someone possessed! Ha, ha, ha!

1. A reference to the Overland Campaign, a series of battles fought in Virginia during May and June of 1864 in the American Civil War.
2. Major General Kuzma Zankisov (1821–1885) was a hero in the struggle for Polish independence from Russia. He was a brave soldier known for dressing entirely in white and he wore a shaggy white hat. He was also the recipient of a white silk badge embroidered with gold presented by "the ladies of Petersburg."
3. Polish revolutionary government.
4. Polish organs of communal local government.

What are they up to? Huh? Also some kind of *sołtys*.[5] Ugh! *Sołtys*! And they even have a *wójt*.[6] A *wójt*. . . ."

With each passing day the conversations at dinner and tea grew shorter and shorter. The most trivial circumstance, the most insignificant occurrence would immediately become a subject of discussion, and every conversation would inevitably end with an argument during which Shchetinin would grow more agitated. Meanwhile Mar'ia Nikolavna would focus on each and every word with intense attention and anxiety; then, apparently dissatisfied with the argument, she would head out into her garden or sit in her own room for hours, staring at one spot. When she encountered Riazanov alone, she would try to talk with him, but usually nothing came of it. Once she asked him: "You probably despise women."

"Why on earth?"

"I don't know, but judging from your conversations, I thought that. . . ."

"No, ma'am," he replied reassuringly. "In general, I don't despise anyone."

That exchange didn't really resolve anything: Riazanov turned to stare out into the field; Mar'ia Nikolavna stood there quite a while looking at his long thinning hair and the tip of his necktie, which was curiously sticking up; then after adjusting her own hair, she walked away.

Another time she encountered him in the garden holding a book. "What are you reading?" she asked Riazanov.

"Some stupid little book."

"Then why are you reading it if it's so stupid?"

"It didn't say on it: *stupid book*."

"Well, but now that you know it is?"

"I've become engrossed and want to know how stupid it really is."

Mar'ia Nikolavna was silent for a while and then asked hesitantly: "Tell me, please . . . do you think my husband's a stupid person?"

---

5. Polish village head.

6. Polish village official.

"No, I don't think that."

"Then why don't you ever agree with him about anything?"

"Because that wouldn't be helpful to either of us."

"Why wouldn't it be helpful for him?" Mar'ia Nikolavna asked hastily.

"Ask him yourself."

"I certainly will." She broke off a twig from an acacia tree, started tearing off its leaves rapidly, and without even notic-ing, began tossing them at his book. Riazanov silently lifted his book, shook the leaves off, and once again set about reading. Mar'ia Nikolavna glanced at him, tossed the twig down, and walked away.

After one such conversation she entered her husband's study and found him at work: he was reviewing some accounts. She glanced around and began searching for something.

"What is it, Masha?" Shchetinin asked.

"No, I thought you were. . . ."

"What do you want?"

"But you're busy."

"What of it? It's nothing. Is there something you want to talk about?"

"Mmm . . . yes. I wanted to ask you. . . ."

"Well, tell me. Sit down. What's on your mind?"

"Nothing. Perhaps Riazanov might come in."

"No; he won't be coming in now. What of it? You don't want to talk about it in his presence, is that it?"

Mar'ia Nikolavna remained silent; Shchetinin tried to embrace her, but she quietly removed his arm and gave his hand a squeeze. It was almost dark in the room; a candle with a lampshade was burn-ing on the desk and lit only his papers and a large bronze inkwell. Through the window, together with a few moths, random phrases of songs floated in along with the soft, muffled voices of people wandering around the courtyard. Mar'ia Nikolavna sat on the sofa; she had turned to one side and was tugging at one of the buttons on the pillow. First she would glance at her husband, as if to say something, then focus back on the button to examine it carefully; then she would pause, but still didn't say anything.

Regarding his wife anxiously, Shchetinin asked, "Well, so? What is it?"

"You see," she began at last. "I've been wanting to ask you for a long time . . . yes . . . about all this. . . . Perhaps I don't understand things. . . ."

"What don't you understand?"

"Why are you always arguing with Riazanov. . . ."

"Well, what of it?"

"Why can't you ever convince him?"

"Only that?"

"Yes, that's it."

"So, that's what you're so upset about?"

"Well, yes."

"Good Lord! I thought, God knows what had happened, but you . . ." said Shchetinin, standing up from the sofa and laughing.

"So, you think it's all nonsense?" Mar'ia Nikolavna asked, jumping up from the sofa and drawing near her husband. "Don't you believe what you say? Therefore, you. . . ."

"What is it? What?" Shchetinin asked, taking a step back. "I don't understand what you mean. How can it be that I don't believe what I say? Do me a favor, explain that to me."

"The explanation's very simple," Mar'ia Nikolavna said, getting more and more agitated. "You argue with Riazanov. Why do you? Because you think that . . . well, because he doesn't think the same way you do. Isn't that right?"

"Yes, indeed."

"Why don't you prove to him that what he thinks is wrong? Why can't you out-argue him? Why not? Why are you so quiet? Tell me! Speak up! Now!" She tugged at her husband's sleeve. "Why don't you answer? So, you do feel he's right. Hmm. Is that it? He's laughing at you, at your every word, and you just get angry. . . . Therefore. . . . Why don't you answer me? You see that I . . . oh, what's this all about?" she suddenly cried out, pushed her husband away, fell onto the sofa, and buried her face in the pillow.

Shchetinin stood in the middle of the room and spread his arms wide. "Dammit all! I don't understand a thing. . . . What's happened to you? Be so good as to tell me," he said, approaching his wife and touching her arm.

"Nothing, nothing's happened to me," she replied as she stood up. "It's only that now I see how mistaken I was, that I . . . that up to now I was mistaken, terribly mistaken," she said, now entirely serene.

"In what? What?"

"You don't know? Do you really think that I didn't understand from all these arguments that you've been trying to deceive me and other people? You could deceive me, of course, but Riazanov catches you on every word; he shows at each and every step that you say one thing but do another. What? You say it's not true? Aha? Well, speak! Ah? That means it's true! You see! It is true!"

Shchetinin paced the room briskly from end to end, shrugging his shoulders.

"Listen," he said, stopping in front of her. "Have you spoken with him?" Shchetinin nodded his head in the direction of the annex of the house.

"I did."

"What did he tell you?"

"He hasn't said anything about this; I didn't even ask him. Everything's clear to me now even without him. You think I don't see that you wanted to make me a housekeeper."

"When was that? When?" Shchetinin asked, approaching his wife. "Masha! What are you saying? My dear! Well, listen to me!"

He sat down next to her and took her hand.

"No, wait," she said, pulling her hand away. "When I was still . . . when you wanted to marry me, what was it you said to me then? Try to remember."

"What did I say?"

"You told me that we'd work together, perform some great feat, which might perhaps destroy us, and not only us, but all those around us. But you said you weren't afraid. If I felt the strength within me, we'd set off together. So I agreed. Of course, at the time I was still foolish; I didn't quite understand what you were saying. I merely felt it and sensed it. I would have followed you anywhere. You knew that I loved my own mother dearly, but I left her. She nearly died of grief, but I left her anyway, because I thought, I believed, that we'd perform some real exploit. And how has it all ended? You haggle with the peasants over every kopeck, while I pickle cucumbers and listen to peasants beating their wives—and I stand there staring at them blankly. I listen and listen, and then go back to pickling cucumbers. If I'd wanted to become what you've turned me into, I'd have married some Siskin or other, and by now maybe I'd have had three children. Then at least I'd know that I was simply a female of the species, a mother; I'd know that I was sacrificing myself for my children, but now. . . . You know that I'd have gladly gone with you to plow the earth, if it'd been necessary for the common good. But now? What am I? I'm Mr. Shchetinin's housekeeper. A housekeeper, pure and simple, who counts every half-kopeck, and worries what will happen if someone eats an extra pound of bread! Or, what if. . . . How disgusting!"

She stood up and wanted to leave, but Shchetinin made a move to stop her. She turned and said to him: "No. I've understood all this for a long time, a very long time, and I've been mulling it over. But up to now I wasn't able to grasp it fully. Well, all these conversations with Riazanov have really helped me. I've been very upset, very agitated. But it was unnecessary. It was all because I buried these thoughts for so long; I tried to talk myself out of it, but do you know what I really should've done? Without saying anything, I should've, I simply should've. . . ."

"Masha!" said Shchetinin in a trembling voice, going up to her and taking her by the arm. "Masha! What are you saying? But . . . well, but . . . I love you. Do you understand that?"

"Yes, and I love you, too," she said, holding back tears. "I understand that you . . . you also . . . made a mistake, but I can't go on like this. Understand? I can't just . . . pickle cucumbers. . . ."

Shchetinin held his head; squeezing his eyes tight, he flung himself onto the sofa.

When he opened his eyes again, Mar'ia Nikolavna was gone.

He looked at the door, stood up, and began pacing the room, his head lowered, his hands clasped behind his back. From his face it was apparent that some new terrible thoughts kept occurring to him; at times these thoughts frightened him, at other times they compelled him without any need to seize various objects lying on tables in the room. He stopped in front of the window, drummed a bit on the glass, then rubbed his finger, and quite automatically traced on the glass: *cucumbers*. Then he quickly wiped that word out; placing both hands on the back of his head, he walked toward the door, but then turned back, grabbed his hairbrush, and began brushing his hair. He did so for a long time, next even brushing the chest of drawers; all of a sudden he tossed the brush aside, sat down on the sofa, and buried his face in his hands. After a few minutes he uncovered his face, rested his elbows on his knees, and stared at the floor. Then he stood up again, walked quietly to the mirror, looked into it, and carefully, without hurrying, but apparently completely unaware, removed his necktie, unbuttoned his vest, started to take off his jacket; then he put his jacket back on once again in such a way that the lining started to tear; at last he left the study. He stopped in the dark corridor in front of his wife's room, and was about to open the door, but it was locked.

"Who's there?" Mar'ia Nikolavna asked.

"May I come in?" Shchetinin asked hesitantly.

"What for?"

Shchetinin was silent. There was no reply from her room. He stood there a while, quietly took his hand away from the handle, and returned to his study. He sat down slowly on the sofa, opened a book, rested his head on his hand, and began looking at it; he carefully scraped off a dead fly stuck between some pages, turned a page without even noticing that the book was upside down, and then got engrossed in reading again.

Half an hour passed. At last he sighed, pushed the book away, looked around, and went to the annex.

Riazanov was lying on his bed staring at the ceiling. A candle was burning on a chair next to him; an open book was lying nearby on the floor.

"What is it?" Riazanov asked him.

"Well, my friend . . . here's what: an unpleasant situation has arisen. . . ."

"What kind of situation?"

Riazanov turned onto one side; Shchetinin stood over him and examined the candle.

"The kind that . . . how can I say it? One, you know, that sometimes happens. . . ."

"Where does it happen?"

"In town. What is it, damnit? What's it called? An assembly. Yes. An assembly of mediators."[7]

"So what?"

"Well, let's go!"

"Do you have business there, or what?"

"What kind of business? What the devil for?"

"Then why are you asking me?"

"I'm asking, don't you see, because. . . ." Shchetinin walked over to the window. "I'm asking, my dear friend," he continued, picking up the book from the floor and leafing through its pages, "so that . . . don't you see, you won't be bored here. I'll be merrier, and so will you. Understand? Yes. One can rot away here in the country. What's so good about it? Right?" said Shchetinin, closing the book and handing it to Riazanov.

Riazanov stared at him fixedly and took the book. "Why are you talking such nonsense?" he asked at last. "Are you ill or what?"

"Yes, my friend; I have a terrible headache. Goodbye!"

Riazanov watched him leave, shrugged his shoulders, opened the book, and began reading.

Shchetinin went back to the house, walked right into his bed-

---

7. One institution of the judicial system established by Alexander II in the legal reforms of 1864, based partly on English, partly on French models.

room, lit a candle, and sat down on a chair next to the bed. Mar'ia Nikolavna's nightgown and bedcap lay on the pillows. The bed remained unwrinkled, just as it had been made up. A carafe of water stood on the little table next to the pillows. Shchetinin poured himself a glass and drank it; glass in hand, he stared at the pillow for a long time; then he placed the glass on the table, adjusted the blanket, and returned to his study.

The next morning the steward came in several times on business, but Shchetinin was still asleep. The samovar was brought in around nine o'clock; Mar'ia Nikolavna went into the dining room to prepare tea; some peasants appeared in the entrance hall. They finally woke Shchetinin and the steward entered his study. The master was sitting at his desk, rubbing his eyes, but didn't understand a thing that was said to him. The steward stood near the door, looked in, took a step forward, bowed, waited a bit, coughed, and decided to speak: "Leksan Vasil'ich."

"Huh?"

"Do you want us to cover the ceilings in the annex or should we wait for you?"

"Wait, wait. . . ."

"So, you want to be there?"

"Well, yes. Of course."

Shchetinin kept rubbing his eyes but it didn't seem to help.

The steward waited a little longer.

Just then, with his elbows resting on the desk, Shchetinin began to doze. The steward coughed once again; Shchetinin winced and opened his eyes.

"What's your order concerning the Kriukov peasants?" the steward asked a bit louder.

"Yes, indeed; yes, my friend. . . ."

"Do we let them have the grove?"

"Sure, let them!"

"The grove's being cleared a little at a time."

"Huh?"

"It's being cleared, I say."

"Well, yes. What else. . . ."

"It'll look better, more cheerful."

"Ah! A very good thing, my friend." Shchetinin smiled and began dozing again.

A few moments later the steward asked: "When will you be coming?"

"Where?"

"To the farm, sir."

"Well, what next? Why the hell should I go there? As though I haven't seen your farm," said Shchetinin in a dissatisfied tone of voice, and lowered his head onto the desk.

"Why are you pestering him?" asked Mar'ia Nikolavna in a low voice from the dining room. "Can't you see he's sleeping?"

"Who's sleeping? Me? That's not true!" Shchetinin said, jumping up from the chair. "I'm not asleep."

The steward was still standing in the doorway. Shchetinin opened his eyes wide, stretched, looked around, frowned, and became thoughtful. "Yes," he uttered, as if remembering something. "That's so. . . ." Then, after noticing the steward, he added: "Here's what, my friend: you . . . how shall I say it? You, my dear friend . . . well, yes; have the horses harnessed quickly," he said, now completely awake. "And, as for that business, we'll see about it later. Go on!"

"Some peasants have also arrived," the steward started to say, pointing at the ones standing in the entrance hall.

"Get rid of them," cried Shchetinin.

Riazanov came in; Shchetinin hurriedly drank a glass of tea and washed his face. During all this time neither of them said a word. As soon as they drove out into the field, Shchetinin fell asleep and slept all the way to town.

CHAPTER V

——

AND IN FACT, THERE WAS AN ASSEMBLY OF MEDIATORS in town and in addition, a peasant fair. Drunken peasants and dressed-up countrywomen wandered the streets; tents and stalls with goods stood on the market square; music was being played and songs were being sung in the makeshift tavern; the sun was baking and a cloud of dust hovered over the crowd of peasants milling in all directions; a police superintendent and his mounted assistant on a pair of dark bay horses made their way among the carts. Stewards and young ladies with bundles and made-up faces mingled in the crowd.

On one side, near the scales, stood six soldiers from the garrison in cloth ties and white canvas uniforms. A captain was pacing up and down in front of them: he was both inspecting and abusing them, while he himself was intoxicated. The soldiers were also drunk and, sighing, examined the passersby with indifference. The open carriage in which the captain had arrived was standing there. He was getting ready to leave, would go up to the carriage several times and lift his leg to get in, but then would return immediately and resume his abuse. On the right flank stood a soldier with a tearful face. He was more intoxicated than the others; standing at attention, he was weeping and didn't take his eyes off his commanding officer.

"I'll sho-o-ow you, you motherfucker, I'll show you," the captain yelled, advancing on the soldier.

"Yes, sir, always ready," the soldier replied, holding out his face.

"Shut up!"

"Yes, sir-r-r-r."

"I'll beat the life out of you!"

"Gladly. . . ."

Smack!

The soldier blinked and thrust his face even further forward. Peasants passing stopped to look. The soldier sobbed and, without wiping away his tears, stared straight into his commander's eyes.

"Ugh! Imbecile," growled the captain, casting a sidelong glance at the soldier and heading for his carriage.

"As you like," cried the soldier.

"Shut up!" roared the captain, rushing back to the soldier.

Landowners rode and strolled through the streets; vodka and snacks were being served in all the houses; the smell of tobacco smoke wafted from open windows together with laughter and the clinking of decanters.

This day had been set for the opening of the renovated noblemen's club, renamed the "united" club, since all classes would now be included. The assembly of mediators was to take place in this building, and consequently both at the gates and on the porch a crowd of peasants had gathered, summoned to town on business by the mediators.

Shchetinin and Riazanov strolled around the fair and then headed for the club. They met some gentry along the way; they were walking in step, in a row of four, embracing and singing a march as they went.

A small, plump landowner marched out in front, brandishing a plan for amicable fraternization instead of his saber.

"Warm greetings, your excellency!" the nobles barked, when they drew even with Shchetinin and then passed him.

"Thanks, lads!" cried a landowner who'd stuck his head out of a window.

"Glad to try. . . ."

"One cup each, for our comrade! Come here!" he cried, waving his arm.

"Right turn ahead—march!" the commander demanded, and the regiment turned into the gates.

A light carriage pulled by a troika of small horses raced down the street. A plump man in a military cap, but sporting a beard, sat in it and waved to Shchetinin. He bowed.

Ladies glanced out of windows and said, indicating Shchetinin and Riazanov: "There they go, those communists."[1]

Shchetinin went along in silence and looked absentmindedly from side to side, responding absentmindedly to the greetings. Standing and lounging near the entrance to the club were the local authorities: elected representatives, peasant-assistants to the police, village elders, and so on. Several of them had settled in the shade and their hats were propped up on the fence. The session of the assembly of mediators had yet to conclude. In the center of the hall stood a large table at which the mediators sat with their chains of office around their necks; the chairman sat at the head of the table. Peasants were crowded around them, as well as stewards and attorneys; the remaining nobles wandered around the hall and, apparently, were bored. Boisterous conversation, laughter, and wisecracks could be heard coming from the buffet.

"Enough!" one landowner said, trying to convince the mediators. "Well, really, you've kept at it long enough! It's time for some vodka."

"Wait," the mediators replied with worried looks. "Don't interfere!"

"Allow me, gentlemen, to read to you," one of the mediators began in a loud voice, turning to the assembly, "a letter that I received several days ago from a landowner, a Mr. Pichugin."

---

1. Used as a term of abuse for social reformers who advocated communities based on common ownership. Sleptsov himself had organized a women's commune in Petersburg in the early 1860s.

"We're listening," replied the chairman and his face assumed a serious look.

The mediator began reading:

"Dear sir, Ivan Andreevich. I do not have the honor of being personally acquainted with you; I do have the honor of relaying the following episode to you. On May 12, 1863, a peasant-proprietor in the small village of Zhdanovka, one Anton Timofeev, came to see me at my estate in a dissolute condition, and insolently demanded from me that I return his countrywomen to him, threatening that if I refused, he would lodge a complaint to mediator of the peace. When I sent word to him through a woman previously indebted to me, Arina Semënova, that according to the terms of the agreement I was able to employ his women all summer,[2] he began to abuse my woman in every way possible, calling her a *bitch* and sticking his tongue out at her. After this kind of thing, why, any pig could spit in my eye without fear of punishment! Of course, now that they're liberated, they can do anything they want. But I won't leave it like this and ask the higher authorities to defend me from peasant oppression and arrogance. No, there'll be too much of that if everyone starts imitating their vulgar behavior. As it is, they've been given everything and we've lost everything. I have the honor of being . . ." and so on and so forth.

"Gentlemen!" cried one of the landowners standing near the table, "gentlemen, who's willing to bet that it was this same Mr. Pichugin who persecuted that fellow, the proprietor, with his dogs?"

"So that's it!"

"Does someone want to bet? I know him. Don't believe what he writes. He's lying; he made it all up himself."

An argument ensued. The assembly, meanwhile, having instructed the mediator to investigate the matter where it occurred, moved on to an examination of a project presented by a woman landowner who wanted to resettle peasants to an arid desert. This lady's attorney, a German, unfolded the plan and placed it on the table in front of the

---

2. The reform of 1861 freed the peasants from serfdom, but at the same time obligated them to continue working for their landowners until 1863.

assembly. The mediators began scrutinizing it: in fact the desert depicted was without water; but, in spite of that, the attorney affirmed that it would still be better for the peasants. They summoned them in. They entered, walking carefully across the polished floor, bowed, and shook their heads. The chairman began explaining the landowner's desire to them and showed them the plan with the plots. The peasants listened and said, "We hear, sir." Only one of them looked askance at the plan, screwed up one eye, and moved his lips. But when asked if they agreed to it, all the peasants suddenly began speaking, made their way up to the plan, and started poking their fingers at it. The agent intervened and asked the chairman to prevent the peasants from soiling the plan. The peasants were forbidden from touching it with their fingers and were ordered to move away from the table.

"Well, my dear fellow, how's the free labor doing?" one landowner asked Shchetinin as he finished his sandwich.

"Not too bad," Shchetinin replied reluctantly.

"Well, thank heavens," said the landowner with a smile. "And are all your peasants in good health, those proprietors, that is? Huh? Are they all praying to God for you? What kind of stone palaces have they built themselves? Huh?"

"How would I know?" Shchetinin replied disgruntledly.

"Yes. Or don't you get into it nowadays? Just so. No, take me. To tell the truth," the landowner added after waiting a while, "I go around thinking about how I could entice my peasants into fulfilling their *corvée*; then I could give them a good scolding; I'd show them who's boss and what's what; then they'd quickly pay their redemption fee. However, the problem is that they're not willing to do it, those rascals, so we're stuck neither here nor there."

"How are you?" said Shchetinin, bowing to another landowner who'd just come from behind the buffet.

"As you can see," he replied. "Having a bite to eat. How can we be? Ha, ha! Ivan Pavlych and I have come back a third time. Yes, the heck with waiting for them," he said, indicating the mediators. "Gentlemen, what's all this about ultimately? Soon there'll be nothing left. They've drunk all the vodka at the buffet and now they're on to the sherry."

"Order them to set the table," said the others.

"A table's needed."

"Gentlemen, drag them away from the table!"

"Hey, you, fetch a pail of water, my man. We'll douse them. It's the only way."

"Ha, ha, ha!"

"No, seriously, gentlemen! What kind of outrage is this? Everyone wants to eat. Whom do you want to surprise?"

"Why even go on with them? Get up, gentlemen! This meeting's over. To hell with it! Drive the peasants away! Hey, you, get outta here!"

Thus concluded the assembly. The mediators folded their documents with worried and exhausted faces, removed their chains of office, stretched, and headed for the buffet.

"Aleksandr Vasil'ich, my dear fellow, have you been here long?" asked one of them approaching Shchetinin. "Let me greet you with a kiss, my friend. *Et, madame votre épouse, comment se porte-t-elle?*"[3]

"Thank you. This is my comrade, Iakov Vasil'ich Riazanov; this is the mediator of the peace in our district, Semën Semënych: get acquainted," said Shchetinin.

"Glad to meet you, very glad," said the mediator, bowing and scraping, and shaking Riazanov's hand. "Ah, I seem to recognize your name, Riazanov. Yes. Now I remember. I served together with your father."

"What was it you served with him, vespers or liturgy?" asked Riazanov.

"What do you mean?"

"I don't exactly know. It must have been all the priests together. Or else, what?"

The mediator looked at Riazanov in bewilderment. "Didn't your father serve in the Grodno hussars?"[4]

---

3. "And madam, how is your wife?" (Fr.)

4. The regiment was created in 1806. Grodno was a Russian city located on the Neman River, close to the borders of Poland and Lithuania.

"No, he served more as a presbyter in villages."

"That is. . . ."

"As a priest, sir."

"Yes. Well, then it's not the same Riazanov I knew," said the mediator in confusion.

"I think it's not the same."

They began setting the table. In anticipation of dinner the nobles strolled in the hall, snacking and chatting.

"Gentlemen, listen to this!"

"Go on!"

"Has anyone heard or read about the *zemstvo*—what on earth is it?"[5]

"Come on, what have you brought up now? Let me kiss you for asking that question!"

"No, wait a moment, my friend, it's not possible to let this go."

"Why isn't it? Come, on, friend, it's better to go and have some vodka. Why even talk about the . . . *zemstvo*? What's it to you?"

"What's it to me? For you daredevils, it means nothing at all, but I have children, my friends. Gentlemen, no, seriously, tell me if someone knows what it's all about!"

"Stop pestering me!"

"Why should I? You probably won't pay for me!"

"Allow me, my dear, I will pay; but let's go together and both have a glass."

"Do me a favor, leave me alone! Ivan Pavlych, you, my good fellow, don't you know? It seems that you read journals."

"What's that?"

"Have you read anything about the *zemstvo*?"

"Of course I have."

"Well, what is it?"

---

5.   One of a system of elected district councils established in Russia in 1864 to
      administer local affairs after the abolition of serfdom.

"I don't know, my dear fellow, so help me God."

"Aren't there any newspapers here?"

"What newspapers? Go ask at the buffet! Hey, you, bring him a serving of newspapers!"

"Damn! They've lapped up all the vodka. At least pour me some rum, will you?"

"So what about the *zemstvo*? Huh? Doesn't anyone know?"

"Ask the marshal of the nobility."[6]

"Marshal, do me a favor and tell me, my friend. I can't get an answer from anyone about what this *zemstvo* is. What kind of animal is it? Is it some sort of tax? Huh?"

"It's, don't you see, it's a kind of. . . ."

"Do you even know yourself?"

"Well, what kind of a question is that? I'm not permitted not to know."

"What did I tell you? No lies! Well?"

"How can I say it, it's a government matter."

"Well, all right. Then don't tell us about it; but the main point, what's the main point of it?"

"Its strength, my friend, is that it's elected."

"I see. Who gets elected?"

"The elected ones."

"Yes. So it's the elected ones who get elected again. Well, and what the hell will they be elected for?"

"They're going to decide that there."

"Yes, yes, yes. What will they discuss?"

"Various matters: the roads, supplying bridges, and so on."

"Yes. That means, the road department. Well, and we are going to pay them money for this? We are, aren't we?"

"Yes."

"Well, marshal, my friend, thanks for telling us. Now let's go down a glass."

---

6.   A chosen representative of the nobility of a district, elected to manage their affairs and represent their interests in local government organs.

A few minutes before dinner, bells rang out in the street and a foam-covered troika of splendid gray steeds halted near the porch. A plump, ruddy young landowner entered the hall wearing an English jacket and carrying a lap robe.

"Petia! My boy! Here he is, the beast! Dear lad! Can you stay for a while?"

"What's going on here? Are the different classes now becoming friends? Ah, you're all clowns! Where are the peasants?"

"What peasants? They're over there, on the porch."

"Then what about the classes?"

"Well, what do you mean, the classes!"

"Why did you tell lies?"

"Who told you a lie? Look and you'll see, Lakov's sitting there. What else do you need?"

In fact, on the sofa sat a merchant with a red nose who was casting his eyes around foolishly.

"Why, that pig's already drunk. Hey, Lakov, my friend, are you soused already?"

"I am," the merchant replied, nodding his head and smiling.

"What an animal!"

"No! It's a fair."

Another merchant peered out from behind the buffet, and, standing in the doorway, bowed servilely, undecided about whether to enter the hall.

"Ah! So you're here, too, you old fart! Why don't you come in?"

"He doesn't dare."

"I don't dare, sir."

"Well, fine, my friend; just stay out there! We'll initiate you after dinner."

"We will, we will. . . ."

The merchant bowed.

They served the soup. People began taking their seats at the table. The merchant Lakov also found a chair.

"So, gentlemen, may I?"

"Sit down, you dummy, go on, sit down."

The merchant sat down. "Hey, waiter, bring us a pitcher of vodka!"

"They're not serving vodka at the table. What do you think? This isn't a tavern," his companions said to the merchant.

"Well, some champagne, then! Damn it all!"

"How much?"

"Half a bottle!"

"Hey, you! Half a bottle! You, peasant! Where are you sitting? Remember!"

"What's all this? We'll order half a dozen bottles. Bring us half a dozen!"

"Yes, sir."

"And something to snack on, something salty. Quick! Hey, shut up. . . ."

"Lakov, behave yourself more moderately," someone shouted at him from the other end of the table.

"I'm being very moderate."

"Gentlemen, have you heard what happened in Saratov?"[7]

"What?"

"They caught the arsonists. Now there's such a mess . . . it turns out that various people were involved. . . ."

"What a mess! Our peasants caught two of them; arrested them, the idiots, and then let them go."

"Well, allow me to inquire," a neighbor, a district teacher, asked Riazanov. "Will they send a telegram?"

"I don't know."

"What's he saying?"

"I'm talking about a telegram, sir."

"What telegram?"

"That is, from all the classes, right now, during dinner. Won't they do it?"

---

7.   An allusion to the fires in Petersburg and other cities, which the government and reactionary press used as a pretext for baiting the opposition.

"No; there won't be any telegram, but Pëtr Mikhailovich will speak—in Latin."

"Ah, really! Petia," cried one mediator, "speak, my friend. A speech today, without fail!"

"That's after dinner," replied Petia.

"No, last week he . . . we were out hunting . . . I almost died laughing: he gathered the peasants together and gave them a speech in Latin."

"Ha, ha, ha!"

After the soup corks began popping and champagne was served.

"Gentlemen, to the uniting of classes! Lakov, do you hear, you dummy?"

"Ah, to hell with you!"

"Ha, ha, ha! But, no cursing, you son of a bitch!"

"'Ustiushka's mother was about to die . . .'" Lakov began reciting.[8]

"We don't ever need to allow those pigs in," some nobles argued. "They let him sit at the table and he put his feet up on it."

"'Die or not, but she passed the time.' What's all this? I paid money for it. . . . Hey, don't we have any money?"

"Ivan Pavlych, to your health," the landowners said, clinking their glasses across the table.

"You should be strung up on a pole," Lakov shouted in the meantime.

"Gentlemen, what's going on?"

"*Mais, mon cher, que voulez-vous donc? C'est un paysan.*"[9]

"Hey, listen here, you peasant," said one landowner to Lakov. "If you, you swine, continue to misbehave, they're going to show you to the door right now."

"You're not worthy to sit at the table with decent people."

Lakov backed down.

---

8. The beginning of a children's teasing rhyme.

9. "What do you expect, my friend? After all, he's a peasant." (Fr.)

"Will you sit quietly?"

"Yes, I will. So help me God. . . . I want to be a scoundrel—quietly."

"Well, then be quiet; no cursing."

"I'll be damned—I didn't curse!"

"Gentlemen, to the well-being of the club," the marshal proposed.

"'Ustiushka's mother . . .'" roared Lakov. "Hey, do we have any money? I'll buy you all, sell you, and then redeem you again."

"No, he's gotten out of hand. He has to be thrown out."

"Here's some money—take it! Hey! Who'll take the money—take it! Three hundred silver rubles . . . for everyone . . . I'm making a donation, to hell with you!"

"Throw him out, out!" the nobles cried.

"Wait," said Lakov. "Give me back the money for four bottles! All right. Well, now throw me out!"

An hour after dinner the nobles wandered around the rooms as if in a dream: everyone was saying something to someone, shouting, singing, and constantly demanding champagne and more champagne. In one room a group was singing a song, but then it turned out to be two groups, but no one was listening; all you could make out was:

"'A goblet of amber. . . .'"[10]

"'So the sun wouldn't bake. . . .'"

"'Long since full up. . . .'"

"'So the lard wouldn't melt.'"

"Gentlemen, what a disgrace! Hurrah! More champagne! Drink, drink, drink! Allow me to tell you! 'So the sun wouldn't. . . .' To hell with you! Hurrah! More champagne!"

At the same time one landowner seated on top of the table was singing in a delicate voice: "'The splen-n-n-did young century, my friends-s-s, is pas-s-s-sing. . . .'"[11]

---

10. Assorted lines from Pushkin's early lyric "The Toasting Goblet" (1816), set to music by Mikhail Glinka.

11. The first line of a popular Russian romance by N. M. Konshin.

"Vo-o-od-ka!" someone suddenly roared in a desperate voice.

The initiation of the merchant Stratonov was taking place in the next room. The judge, sitting in his armchair, was uttering some words and a choir was repeating them. Two mediators held the merchant Stratonov by the arms and made him bow down to the judge. The merchant bowed down to the ground and asked for the judge's hand. He covered him with the flap of his jacket and pronounced the words "*Axios, axios*";[12] the choir echoed the words; a third mediator waved a chain, as if it were a censer.

Shchetinin and Riazanov went out onto the porch. It was growing dark. Near the gates of the club their harnessed carriage was waiting for them. One landowner was standing in the courtyard, his head leaning up against a wall, painfully paying for his dinner.

Some young boys were standing in front of the illuminated windows engaged in the following conversation among themselves:

"Don't go in! The mediator's in there."

"It's an assembly."

"He'll eat you up."

"Who will?"

"The mediator. You watch out! Watch out! He's so terrible! Look, lads! His teeth! What teeth he has!"

"Hurrah!" the nobles shouted in the club and tossed empty bottles out the windows.

Drunken peasants wandered the streets. The fair had ended.

"What was it you were starting to tell me when I arrived, do you recall? About some social matter?" Riazanov asked his comrade when they had driven out into the field.

"No, leave it alone, I beg you; do me a favor, leave it alone," replied Shchetinin.

---

12. "[He is] worthy, [he is] worthy" (classical Greek). Words sung by the choir in the Orthodox ritual of ordaining a priest.

CHAPTER VI

———

SHCHETININ AND RIAZANOV RETURNED FROM TOWN that night, sometime after midnight; Riazanov went off to the annex, while Shchetinin went right to his study, got undressed, read through some letters, and scanned the newspaper; resting his elbows on the table, he fell into thought.

Several minutes passed.

"Won't you be eating?" the footman asked gloomily.

"Huh?"

Shchetinin seemed to come to.

"Won't you be eating?" the footman repeated in the same gloomy tone of voice.

"No, I won't."

The footman was about to leave.

"Wait! What . . . ah . . . do you know if the mistress's already gone to bed?" Shchetinin asked, flustered and scrutinizing the newspaper.

"Don't know, sir."

"Ah . . . is she . . . well?"

"Don't know, sir."

Shchetinin frowned and regarded the footman distrustfully: the footman, placing one hand behind his back, holding the master's boots in his other, stood near the lintel and glowered at him.

"Why do you have the habit," Shchetinin began in irritation, "of saying 'Don't know, sir,' or 'By no means, sir'? Damn it all: only soldiers talk like that."

The footman shifted his weight from leg to leg and continued staring at his master in silence.

"It seems I've asked you before—but no, you don't listen!"

Silence.

"For the last time I ask you: don't talk like that, do me a favor!"

"Yes, sir."

Shchetinin waved his arm dismissively.

"Go away! Out!" he said in an imploring tone of voice.

The footman withdrew.

Shchetinin folded the newspaper, slapped it with his palm to flatten it, and was about to start reading; but he immediately began drumming his fingers on the table and staring at the candlestick. It was quiet; he could hear the horses being unharnessed in the courtyard. . . . Suddenly somewhere in the distant rooms there was a sound of knocking and the rustling of a woman's dress. . . . Shchetinin shuddered, raised his head, and began listening: the floor creaked . . . the rustling came closer and closer . . . now she made her way into the hall . . . her dress brushed against a chair . . . and she entered the dining room. . . .

"Forgive me, my dear," said Mar'ia Nikolavna, coming into the study.

Shchetinin rushed to her and grabbed her hands stretched toward him.

"I caused you distress—forgive me! Now I myself can see that you're a good man after all, yes, a good man."

Shchetinin rested his hands on her shoulders and looked tenderly into her eyes.

"What I said to you was completely unnecessary. I'm very sorry. . . ."

She said all this in a tender but firm voice; there were tears in her eyes.

"Well, that's enough, quite enough," said Shchetinin, kissing her on the head.

"No, you know, right after you left, I started thinking, and I've been thinking all day and all night. . . . I've rethought all my ideas."

"Let's sit down," he said, embracing his wife and leading her over to the sofa. "Well, and what did you come up with?"

He sighed, laid his head on her shoulder, and closed his eyes. "You certainly managed to mistreat me!" he said.

"Forgive me!"

"Well, it's nothing, really. Mere trifles. No, I'd already imagined that. . . . Tell me, however, tell me all!"

"What did you imagine?"

"It's all nonsense. Let bygones be bygones. So what else is there to say? But you tell me: what happened to you?"

"How can I say it? I don't know. It seems that it was nothing special; just, all of sudden it seemed that—that the medical treatments and the housekeeping I do, that all of it was terribly stupid."

"But why? But why hadn't that ever occurred to you before?"

"Before? You see? How can I explain it to you? Up until now I've still been waiting for something, waiting up to the present moment; I wasn't paying attention, not thinking about anything; I merely believed that for some reason it was necessary. You'd said to me, a long time ago: 'Masha, please keep house!' Well, so I did. Then some sick peasants came and you said to me, 'Masha, you should go and see what's wrong with them.' So I started treating them. Well, and that was that. That's how I kept on living. . . . It's as if I was dreaming all that time. And then suddenly these arguments began."

"So, that means. . . ."

"What?"

"No, nothing, nothing. So, then what?"

"At first it seemed that he did it on purpose: then once, you recall, he was advising you to go to court with the peasants? Why, he was making fun of you then. I didn't know what to do: I was simply ready to kill him. Only I didn't say anything to you, but kept reflecting on that conversation, remembering every word of it. . . . But it was all true."

"What was?"

"What he was saying. It was true, wasn't it?"

"Mmm. . . ."

"No, really, think about it: what are we really doing? Land-owners remain landowners. This bothered me terribly. Well, let's suppose, you keep on saying you're a good model, right? You want to show them, well, I don't know what. No, but what am I doing here?"

Shchetinin made no reply. Frowning, he looked out the window and twisted the tassel of his dressing gown. It was starting to grow light outside.

"I remembered," Mar'ia Nikolavna began again, after a little while, "I remembered how at first we talked about various sacri-fices; well now I've looked around: what kind of sacrifices are we making? It's just for amusement. Whether I do what I do or not—it really doesn't matter. And what sort of occupation is it anyway? Ordering dinner, sending clothes to the laundry—this would all happen even without me. And giving a peasant a bandage: I don't even know what I'm doing. Maybe he'll even be worse off as a result. I never studied to become a doctor and I have no skills. So what can I do?"

"Well, tell me instead what you've come up with," interrupted Shchetinin.

"Here's what," she said, placing her finger on her cheek, as if staring at something. "Now I've understood everything. And you're not to blame at all."

Shchetinin raised his brows slightly.

"Do you recall then how you fussed with the peasants, so that they'd . . . what's it called?"

"Well, yes; yes, indeed," Shchetinin said impatiently.

"So that everything they had would be held in common. What's it called?"

"It doesn't matter. So what are you thinking now?"

"Wait a moment. Don't interrupt me! What did I want to say? Yes. You made a mistake then, right?"

"I did," Shchetinin replied quietly.

"But you wished them well?"

"Yes. . . ."

"Then why didn't it work?"

"Because they're fools," Shchetinin retorted abruptly.

Mar'ia Nikolavna paused.

"They don't understand their own good," added Shchetinin; raising up on his elbow, he reached for a pillow.

"Then why are you angry with them?" Mar'ia Nikolavna asked in surprise.

"I don't intend to be angry. Why should I be angry at them?"

"Well, yes. They're not to blame for the fact that they don't understand. They were making a mistake. You also made a mistake. They have to be taught, then they'll understand. Isn't that right?"

"Of course," Shchetinin replied, after some reflection. "But who's going to teach them? Don't tell me you'll do it?" he asked, raising his head.

"Yes, me. Why are you looking at me? Well, yes. I'll teach them. I'll gather the children and start a school. Haven't I come up with a good idea?"

Shchetinin lowered his head again onto the pillow and said: "Of course. Why not? But I don't know. . . ."

"What don't you know? Whether I can carry out this scheme?"

"Exactly. Can you? You'll need tremendous patience. . . ."

"Don't worry. As far as patience is concerned, I . . . besides, Riazanov's here—he's staying with us all summer. He'll help me and explain how to do it all."

"Riazanov? Yes." Shchetinin winced. "No, it's better not to turn to him about this."

"Why not?"

"Just so. In general, he. . . ."

"What?"

"In general . . . he regards all this in an odd way."

Mar'ia Nikolavna became thoughtful. "Have you ever talked to him about this?"

"No, I haven't, but it seems to me, judging from. . . ."

"No. It can't be. He's not like that. However, I'll have a talk with him about it."

"Yes. Well, so, does that mean," said Shchetinin, raising himself up and looking into Mar'ia Nikolavna's face, "does that mean that you're not angry? That's the main thing."

"No. I wasn't angry even then. That's not what it was. So, how were things in town?"

"In town? What a disgrace! They were all drunk as skunks. That's all there was to it. However, it's growing light."

"Indeed, it is," said Mar'ia Nikolavna, getting up. "I'll start tomorrow. First, I'll have a chat with Riazanov. . . ."

"Yes, yes. Good idea."

"And then . . . I'll start. Only then. . . . Wait!"

Shchetinin wanted to embrace her.

"Only I'll have to get some books."

"We will, we'll get whatever's needed."

"You went into town. Ah, I was so foolish!"

"Why?"

"You could've bought supplies there."

"So what? We can order them."

"So tomorrow you'll. . . . Stop it! Send for them tomorrow!"

"I will. Good Lord, I'm so tired!" said Shchetinin, stretching out. "Well, time for sleep!"

CHAPTER VII

————

THE NEXT DAY SHCHETININ GOT UP BEFORE ALL THE
others, drank his tea, and left for the farm for the whole day.

Mar'ia Nikolavna waited at the samovar a long time for
Riazanov to appear; at last she sent for him to the annex—it turned
out that he'd set off at first light and had yet to return. She was
about to go out into the garden, but suddenly returned home. Coming into her room, she opened her little work table, took out the
cuffs she was mending, picked up a needle, and started sewing; then
she ripped out those stitches, pulled out the needle, tore off the
end of the thread, and lowered her hands onto the work. She sat
there for about half an hour, having turned to one side, running
her fingers over her dress in deep thought; only her eyes moved
slowly from one thing to another, not stopping on any one thing,
nor expressing anything specific, except a single vague thought that
gave her no peace. Dreary light from the window entered through
the green curtain and fell palely onto one side of her handsome but
already melancholy face, faintly defining her cheek, her temple with
its immobile brow, and her dark braid thrown back.

————

The maid entered.

"What is it, Polia?" Mar'ia Nikolavna asked, casting a fleeting glance at her.

"Do you want me to sew the blouse or simply baste it for now?"

"It doesn't matter. You'll see which is better."

The maid made no reply.

"Well, start sewing it, all right?"

"They've brought in a girl," the maid said with a smile.

"What girl?"

"Her mother's brought her, a peasant girl. She's sick." The maid chuckled.

"Why are you laughing?"

"It's very funny. The girl has something in her ear. . . ." The maid started laughing again.

"What does she have in her ear?"

"A pea that's growing."

"How's that?"

"Go and see for yourself. The children were playing tricks as usual, and they put a pea in her ear; and it started growing there. If you look, you can see a sprout sticking out."

It turned out that the girl really did have a pea sprout growing out of her ear. Mar'ia Nikolavna removed it with a pin and poured some lamp oil into the girl's ear. The countrywoman pulled four eggs from her bosom and gave them to Mar'ia Nikolavna.

"What's this for? You needn't."

"Well!" said the woman, giving them to her anyway.

"No, really, you don't need to."

"Well! Never mind."

The woman tried to catch hold of her hand.

"Ah, what are you doing? I told you I won't take them," said Mar'ia Nikolavna, hiding her hands.

"Oh? Well, look here. Or take them! Why not? It's nothing."

"She won't take them! You silly woman! She's telling you," added the maid with a laugh.

"But we have no money. What money could we have?"

Mar'ia Nikolavna smiled.

"Or I can bring you some wild strawberries."

"You don't need to bring me anything."

"Well, thank you very much," the woman said, bowing. "Kiss the mistress's hand," she said to her daughter. "Ask for her hand! Wipe your nose first! Say, 'Madam, may I kiss your hand?' Go on, now!"

"No, no; that's not necessary either," said Mar'ia Nikolavna, embarrassed. "Better if you just listen to me."

"Huh?" The woman wiped her own nose.

"What village are you from?"

"You mean, us?"

"Well, yes."

"We're from Kamenskaia."

"That's not far, is it?"

"Nearby. Just across the river."

"How old's the little girl?"

"The girl? She's just turned eight."

Mar'ia Nikolavna leaned over to the girl and took hold of her chin. The little girl looked up suddenly and grabbed her mother's skirt.

"What's your name?" Mar'ia Nikolavna asked the girl.

The girl was silent.

"Why don't you say anything, you silly girl?" her mother said to her. "Tell her: 'Fros'ka, ma'am.'[1] Go on!"

"Fros'ka," whispered the girl, grabbing her mother with both arms and burying her nose in her mother's stomach.

"Listen, my dear," Mar'ia Nikolavna said to the woman with sudden decisiveness and smiled. "Give her to me and I'll teach her."

The countrywoman looked at Mar'ia Nikolavna and also smiled; leaning over the girl, she said: "There, do you hear what the mistress says? She'll teach you, she says. You hear: don't be naughty! If you get naughty, she'll teach you."

---

1. Diminutive form of the girl's name Efrosin'ia.

The girl glanced at Mar'ia Nikolavna and then immediately hid her face again.

"Ah, no. You don't understand," Mar'ia Nikolavna said hurriedly. "I'm not saying this for fun. Really, let me teach her."

"Oh, mistress! What will you think of next?" the maid said with a laugh.

The countrywoman stared at them in bewilderment.

"I'll teach her to read and write," Mar'ia Nikolavna explained to the woman.

"What's she need that for?" asked the woman, not understanding.

"So she'll be literate: she'll know how to read and write, count, and when something's needed, she can write a letter. . . ."

The maid chuckled into her hand.

"You're so strange! What's so funny?" Mar'ia Nikolavna observed, flaring up.

"Oh, I just don't know," said the woman, smiling and looking at the maid.

"What's there not to know? It's very simple," Mar'ia Nikolavna said quickly.

"Oh, no. Leave her alone. . . . No, please, madam."

"Why?"

"No, for the love of God," the woman said, bowing low. "What can you expect from her? She's just a child."

The woman held on to the child, as if someone wanted to take her away. The girl suddenly began crying.

"Maybe you're afraid that she won't be all right here?"

"No, please, madam! She's my only girl. If you want, I can bring you a chicken for treating her."

Mar'ia Nikolavna stood before the woman in silence, smiling sadly; she looked at her and said: "There's no need. I don't want either a chicken or your little girl. Calm down!" She went back to her room.

After waiting a little while she went out onto the porch with her parasol in hand and set off for the servants' quarters.

In the servants' quarters there was a strong smell of cabbage soup and hot rye bread, which were covered over with a towel perched high on a shelf. The coachman was sitting by the window smoking a pipe; the cook was about to take off her shoes and had rested one foot on a bench; a piglet wandered across the floor, munching here and there; next to the coachman, on the same bench, sat a two-year-old little girl who was digging with a large wooden spoon in an empty pot and flies were flying out, buzzing loudly.

The coachman said to the girl, touching her with his pipe: "Grushka!"[2]

"Mm!" replied the girl with annoyance.

"What's that you have?"

"Mmmm!"

"What do you have there?"

"Mm-ma-ma!" cried the girl, slapping the spoon against the pot.

"Hey, you pest, why are you bothering the child?" yelled the cook.

Just then Mar'ia Nikolavna entered. The coachman stood up and hid the pipe behind his back; the cook also stood and straightened up. Mar'ia Nikolavna greeted them, looked around, and said: "It really smells in here!"

The coachman and the cook made no reply. Mar'ia Nikolavna went up to the little girl, stroked her head, and asked: "Is this Grushka?"

"Yes, ma'am," the cook confirmed with a bow.

"Hmm. She's little," Mar'ia Nikolavna said in a low voice; she stood there a few minutes longer, glanced at the stove, and observed that there were a lot of cockroaches.

"Quite a few, ma'am," said the coachman.

"You could get rid of them."

"We did, ma'am," replied the cook.

"It would be better for you," added Mar'ia Nikolavna.

"That's fair," confirmed the coachman. "Even for cleanliness."

---

2.   Diminutive form of the girl's name Agrafen'ia.

"God knows! I don't know what to do about them," said the cook, looking at the cockroaches with despair.

"The best way is with boiling water," said the coachman, approaching the stove.

Having said this, he tossed one cockroach on the floor and squashed it with his foot. "They really hate it when you scald them. They croak at once."

"Well, yes," Mar'ia Nikolavna replied distractedly. "Where's the cabinetmaker?" she asked suddenly.

"He must be with Ivan Stepanych, repairing a violin, I think," the cook answered.

"What violin? They're makin' a cage for the siskin," said the coachman.

"There, you see, it's a birdcage and I thought it was a violin," the cook corrected herself.

"They're playing around in the shed," added the coachman.

Mar'ia Nikolavna went out to the courtyard and sent the coachman to fetch the cabinetmaker.

The cabinetmaker came, removed the strap from his head, and bowed.

"Listen," Mar'ia Nikolavna said to him. "Could you possibly make me a table?"

"Why not? I can, ma'am," said the cabinetmaker after some thought.

"A simple one, you understand, very simple."

"Yes, ma'am. How big should it be?"

"About this big," she said. She showed him using her parasol on the ground.

The cabinetmaker watched and said: "All right. I can, ma'am."

"And two benches like this, long ones."

"That's no trouble at all. I'll use a special saw and then insert the legs into the groove."

"Well, I don't understand any of that."

"I need all the boards to be an inch and half thick," said the cabinetmaker, indicating with his two fingers.

Afterward Mar'ia Nikolavna went to the annex where Riazanov was staying and ordered that one unoccupied room should be cleared of all its clutter and cleaned; then she herself went along the road to the village. The sun was scorching; she walked quickly, her skirt swaying from side to side, and she squinted to see ahead. Not far from the church she ran into an old tradesman who had lived there for a while. He was coming from the mill with fishing poles on his shoulder and was carrying some gudgeon tied to a rope. "My greetings to you, madam," he said, bowing low.

"Ah, hello!"

"Are you out for a stroll?"

"Yes."

"Splendid, ma'am."

"It seems you've been fishing."

"What can I do, ma'am; I love to fish."

"How's your family?"

"Thank the Lord, ma'am—thank heavens."

"What are your children doing? Where's the eldest?"

"He's studying, ma'am."

"Where?"

"Do you know the village of Komzino? Well, he's an apprentice at the shopkeeper's. He himself wanted my Fedia to be there and called us in. We go. 'What,' I say, 'will your situation be?' 'Our situation,' he says, 'will be this: at first,' he says, 'we won't propose anything; then we'll see,' he says. 'If he works hard, we'll propose something.' My wife and I thought about it for a while: well, instead of hanging about and fooling around, let him learn. So we sent him."

"Well, and the younger one?"

"His mama's pet. The little one's still at home with his mother. He's also studying, comforting his parents."

"Who's teaching him?"

"His mother is."

"Is he a willing student?"

"Very. And these days, I can tell you, it's not that we have to beat him; we don't lay a finger on him."

"So how do you do it?"

"We use a spice cookie, ma'am. A spice cookie, and that's all it takes, ma'am. His mother holds up a spice cookie: 'Well, now,' she says, 'Misha,[3] read the prayer to the Mother of God!' He sits right down, picks up his book, and reads the prayer. His mother taught him so well, he devoted himself to it; believe it or not, he learned the whole alphabet in a week."

"Is that so! Goodbye!"

"Goodbye, ma'am."

Mar'ia Nikolavna went a little further. The village was completely empty; the old women sitting at the gate stood up and bowed low from a distance. A group of children lay underneath a barn, where a jackdaw was hopping around, one leg fastened to a string. Mar'ia Nikolavna looked under the barn and asked: "What are you doing here?"

The children hid from her. She leaned in further and looked at them—they tried to hide behind one another.

"Come and see me later and I'll give you some treats," she said to them in a friendly voice.

They were silent.

"So, will you come? Why are you tormenting that jackdaw?" she asked, not waiting for their reply.

From under the barn, someone yanked the rope; the jackdaw cried out, limping on one foot, and then hid under the barn.

Mar'ia Nikolavna stood there for a few moments, sighed, and then left. She paused at the priest's house and wanted to open the gate; a dog was barking in the courtyard, but the gate was locked from the inside and wouldn't budge.

"Who's there?" asked the priest in a disgruntled voice.

"It's me, Mar'ia Nikolavna."

"Ah, excuse me, madam. Please come in!"

The priest was wearing only a short caftan with his sleeves

---

3. Diminutive form of the boy's name Mikhail.

rolled up; he was hurrying and continued making excuses as he led Mar'ia Nikolavna into the sitting room.

"I've only come to see you for a minute," she said upon entering. "Hello, dear."

The priest's wife greeted her and suddenly set about clearing the table.

"I seem to be interrupting."

"No, never mind. Please! You're doing us an honor. I've been busy with household chores here. . . . God's allowed our cow to calve; well, you know, I do everything myself. . . . I'm everything: the master and the grandmother. Ha, ha, ha! What's to be done?"

Mar'ia Nikolavna smiled.

"It's a little awkward, you know, in front of the common folk," the priest added in a low voice. "Since, so to say, I'm a servant of the church, well, it's, don't you know, a little odd. It's a temptation for simple people."

"I've come to see you about a certain matter, father," began Mar'ia Nikolavna.

"Shall we put up the samovar?" asked his wife.

"No, no; thank you. Here's what it is, father. . . ."

"What can I do for you, madam? Pardon me, for heaven's sake, for looking like this. I'll put on my cassock."

"Why on earth? Don't bother."

"I can't, ma'am. Everything, you know, demands decorum."

The priest went behind the curtain, put on his cassock, smoothed his hair, cleared his throat, and finally came out again and said: "Hello, again."

"Father, I've come to talk with you," Mar'ia Nikolavna began hastily. "We have a school here in the village. . . ."

"Yes, ma'am."

"Peasant children study there. Here's what I've decided: I'd like to teach them myself."

"What do you mean, ma'am?" The priest leaned back and squinted.

"Simply to teach them to read and write; well, in general, what I myself know: geography, arithmetic. . . ."

"Hmm, yes, ma'am," said the priest, thinking about it. "Well then? Just as you like, ma'am. Of course. . . ."

"You see, I'd like to find something to do; or else, what am I? I don't do anything. And time is passing . . . and this would be of some use."

"Without doubt," said the priest, staring at the floor.

"Well, I could teach the girls needlework. . . . Still, something or other."

"Of course, ma'am, of course. But, don't you see. . . . The clerk's conducting school now. He's not a very wealthy man; well, and the peasants can't really pay much: some flour or grain, each gives what he can."

"Ah, of course, I'll teach without payment," Mar'ia Nikolavna said, interrupting him.

"No, ma'am, I mean about the clerk; you see, it really provides him with help; he's a poor man; and, if the children are going to study with you. . . ."

Mar'ia Nikolavna was about to reflect on this, but immediately had a thought and said: "Yes. But that doesn't matter. He can be paid. It's no trouble."

"As you wish," said the priest and spread his arms.

After sitting there a little while longer, Mar'ia Nikolavna stood up and left.

"She's a hard one to figure out," said the priest, taking off his cassock.

"Who?" asked his wife, not hearing what he said.

"That one."

"What about her?"

"She's a nuisance, I say."

"Oh!"

"It's the same stallion who's inciting her; he's the one, for sure."

"As God's holy."

After returning from the priest, Mar'ia Nikolavna dropped in at the annex again and paused in the doorway; the cook, the hem of her dress hitched up, was on her hands and knees washing the floor. Mar'ia Nikolavna waited a bit, examined the walls, asked for the window to be opened, and then entered the office. "Have they brought the newspapers?" she asked, entering.

"What, ma'am?" shouted Ivan Stepanych, wearing only a vest, poking his head out of his room, and he withdrew again.

"Did Aleksandr Vasil'ich bring the newspapers from town yesterday?"

"Yes, ma'am," Ivan Stepanych replied, entering the room now wearing his jacket. "They've defeated the Kokandians, and taken those Englishmen away from them,"[4] he explained, removing some fuzz from his jacket.

"What Englishmen?"

"Or maybe it was Italians. Damned if I know. Some Europeans or other. Military prisoners. Well, meanwhile, they really clobbered them."

"So you say," Mar'ia Nikolavna observed distractedly.

"Yes, ma'am," added Ivan Stepanych. "Now all's calm."

"So, is Iakov Vasil'ich home?" Mar'ia Nikolavna asked.

"Yes, I am," Riazanov replied from behind the partition.

"May I come in?"

"Do!"

"I haven't been here once to see you," she said, entering the room. She sat down and looked around. "It's not bad here."

"Yes, not bad, but there are lots of fleas."

"I want to start a school."

"I see! Well, that's good."

"A small one, you know, for now."

"Small?"

"For now."

"Yes. For now, and then a bigger one?"

_____

4. Refers to a Russian military action against the Khanate of Kokand in what is now Uzbekistan.

"Then, perhaps, a bigger one."

"Yes, yes, yes."

Riazanov stood up and paced the room quietly; Mar'ia Niko-lavna followed him with her eyes.

"A school," he said to himself; and pausing in front of Mar'ia Nikolavna, he asked: "Why, exactly, do you wish to start one?"

"Why?"

"That is, with what aim?"

"What a strange question! The usual reason: it's useful."

"Really."

Riazanov paced the room from corner to corner twice more.

"And soon?"

"What soon?" Mar'ia Nikolavna asked quickly.

"You'll start a school?"

"I want to begin tomorrow. You see, I'd like to do it as soon as possible."

"I see. No delay."

"I've already made all the preparations and discussed it with the priest."

"Yes. You've discussed it already?"

"I did."

"Aha. So, why stop?"

"It hasn't stopped, only. . . ."

"What?"

"I'd like to know . . . your opinion."

"About schools? In general, I'm in favor of them. They're use-ful."

"No, I'd like to ask you what you think about my school."

"But it doesn't exist yet. Or, do you want to know my opinion about the fact that you want to start a school?"

"Well, yes, yes. What do you think?"

"What can I think? Now I know you've decided you want to start a school; well, and you will start one. Then I'll know that you wanted to start a school and you did. Now I don't know anything more; consequently, I have nothing to think about."

"And if I ask you to think about it . . ." said Mar'ia Nikolavna, blushing slightly.

"That's still not a reason," replied Riazanov, sitting down opposite her. "Why a school, how come a school, for what purpose— all that's unknown. You yourself don't even know exactly why you want to start a school. So you say, it's useful. Well, fine. But there's lots of useful things on this earth. And there are all sorts of uses."

"Therefore, you regard me," said Mar'ia Nikolavna after a little thought, "as unsuited for this project?"

"I don't regard you as anything. How can I judge what I don't know?" Riazanov stood up again and began pacing. "What sort of books do you have?"

"Various." She picked up one book, opened it, and read the title. "Is this a good book?"

"It depends. For you, it might be good."

"What's written in it?"

"A great deal, but it can all be summarized in a few words."

"What are they?"

"'If you wish to build a temple, take measures beforehand so that the enemy's cavalry doesn't turn it into a stable.'"

"Nothing else?"

"The rest is nonsense."

"Well, then I won't read it."

"As you like."

After this conversation Mar'ia Nikolavna went home and stayed in her room until the evening.

CHAPTER VIII

———

"WITH SUCH HUMANE TREATMENT, SO HELP ME GOD, we'll be completely infested with lice," cried Ivan Stepanych in the morning, hurling something and racing from one corner to another in his office. "You treat them so humanely, so compassionately, as if in fact they had a thousand souls; meanwhile, here sits a man without a shirt to wear."

"What are you grumbling about?" Riazanov asked him through the partition.

He was drinking tea in his own room.

"For pity's sake, it's simply a disaster. The laundress isn't washing the clothes—I've nothing to wear. Look here, if you please," said Ivan Stepanych, entering Riazanov's room. "Greetings! Would you care to regard the fact that I'm wearing this shirt for the second week in a row? Have you ever seen anything like it? Well, it'd be all right in winter, but judge for yourself: it's summertime. An active man sweats. Damn it all," he said, rushing around the room. "Laundress! Huh!? What a swine! Have you seen her?"

"No, I haven't."

"Just ponder this! They brought her here from Moscow. She's the worst sort of scum, just imagine. . . . Probably thinks to herself: 'I do a woman's work.' Huh? She washes my long underwear, and she thinks . . . about what? A woman's work. . . . Huh?"

Riazanov smiled. "Would you like some tea?"

"I myself don't drink it. It's not good for me. And now, she wants to start a school. . . . Ah, you! They'll put it here. There'll be lots more lice! Huh? No, it's not much now, but if you'd seen it before, when he just got married—then it was even more humane treatment! They sat without dinner for three days because of it. The peasants were so completely drunk. . . . One of them bent down to pick up his boots and right there and then . . . he pukes. Stench all over the house. Good Lord! Squabbles every day! What book is that you have? Is it interesting?"

"Listen," Riazanov said to him, without listening. "Why do you beat your dog?"

"Why? I have to. I tell her: 'Tancred, *sauté!*'[1] But she doesn't obey: '*Sauté*, damn you, mutt!' Then she just tucks her tail between her legs and slinks away under the barn. She's such a vile creature. How can I not beat her?"

"No, don't! There's a new fashion these days—not to beat your dogs."

"Now you're talking about humane treatment for dogs. I know. It's all nonsense. If I don't beat her, that devil won't fetch."

"She will."

"You must be thinking about a pointer, an English one. They, the devils, are born fetchers; they have tails like this, standing straight up. Their mother nurses them, and their tail stands up straight."

"What are you talking about? It was a plain mongrel—you know, they're so shaggy."

"So?"

"I've seen them myself."

"So help you God?"

---

1. Jump! (Fr.)

"So help me God."

"Fetches."

"Dances, and fetches, and plays dead. Whatever you like."

"Plays dead? Ah, damn it all! That's amusing. What's it like—tell me!"

"It's a very simple trick: you don't give her anything to eat, nothing at all until she does it. You starve her with hunger; then you take a stick and put a piece of meat on the end, like this—and you say, 'Sauté!' She looks and looks . . . the only thing she can do to get it is jump; then you give her the meat. If you do that three times—then she'll jump even without the piece of meat."

"Well, yes. So that's it," said Ivan Stepanych, considering. "It must be true."

"Absolutely."

After he finished his tea, Riazanov went into the house and found Mar'ia Nikolavna at work in the study; she was sitting on the floor, surrounded by books and covered in dust. He paused in the doorway and asked: "Isn't Aleksandr Vasil'ich here?"

"He'll be back soon," she replied cheerfully. "Hello!" She was about to extend her hand to him, but suddenly hesitated. "Ah, no; I can't shake your hand," she said laughing. "You see, how dusty I am!"

"Well, never mind," said Riazanov and sat down on the sofa.

Mar'ia Nikolavna was sorting through the books on the floor, hastily scanning them and laying some aside. It was very warm in the room; flies were buzzing around her face and into her mouth; she swatted them away quickly, without, however, interrupting her sorting even for a moment. The cook came in for some sugar—without looking, she gave him the keys[2] and then, with the same focused attention, returned to her work. Riazanov picked up from the floor the first book he happened upon and opened it: it was a copy of *Library for Reading* from 1845.[3] He put it down and grabbed

2. Sugar was usually kept under lock and key in a cabinet.

3. *A Russian Journal for Belles Lettres, Science, Art, Commerce, News and Fashions*, published monthly in Petersburg from 1834 to 1865.

another: *Notes of the Fatherland* from 1852.[4] After looking through a dozen or so more, he was satisfied; he picked up a newspaper that was lying on the table and began reading.

"Have you read these books?" Mar'ia Nikolavna asked him.

"I have. What of it?"

"I read them before, too, but now I've started searching to try to make sense of them."

"What sort of sense?"

"You see, I'd like to read as much as possible about the education of the people."

"Ah! What for?"

"So I can teach."

"Yes! That school, right? Well, you've gotten your hands dirty for nothing: you won't find anything there."

"No, I've already found several articles and set them aside. Here, you see?"

Riazanov took the issues of the proffered journals, all dating the end of the 1850s.

"What have you found, some journal articles?"

Mar'ia Nikolavna stood in front of him waiting.

"Some journal articles," repeated Riazanov.

"Well, yes, articles about the education of the people. Here's one, and there's another. You see? This one's also about schools for the common people. I found a lot of them; how can you say there aren't any?"

"That's not what I'm talking about. Of course, there are all sorts of articles here: and there must be some about the education of the people; but what's written here isn't at all what you need."

Mar'ia Nikolavna, holding the books in her hands, looked at Riazanov in consternation.

"Listen, I don't understand what you just said. What do you mean, it isn't what I need?"

---

4. The leading journal of the Westernizers published in Petersburg from 1839 to 1884.

"It's not what you need," replied Riazanov. "You're searching by the titles, right?"

"Naturally, by the titles. How else can I do it?"

"Well, then you'll never find anything. It makes no difference what title they have. It doesn't mean a thing."

"Why not?"

"You understand that it doesn't mean anything if a signboard proclaims 'Russian Truth' or 'White Swan.' So you go in looking for a white swan, and it's a tavern. In order to read and understand these books, you need considerable experience," said Riazanov, getting up. "If an inexperienced person picks up a book, in fact he'll think he sees white swans: and schools, courts, constitutions, prostitution, the Magna Carta, and the devil knows what else . . . and if you look closely at it, well, you'll see it's all just . . . an attempt to sell you stuff."

Riazanov wanted to leave.

"No, wait a bit," Mar'ia Nikolavna said, blocking his way. "Tell me first what's been said in them about schools."

Riazanov sat down on the sofa again. "What schools? The matter concerns something even closer than that. 'School'! That's a misprint. Wherever the word 'school' appears, you should read 'skin.'[5] One person writes: it's very difficult, he says, to safeguard our schools; he meant to say: our skins. Another writes: it'd be a good thing, he says, to insulate them in the manner of Western schools, so that they aren't blighted by various influences. Do you see? And a third person writes: incense, you have to fumigate with incense, he says, more frequently. I experienced it myself, he says—it's the best remedy. It's all about 'skins.' Well, naturally, since it's so very clever, people don't understand this and think that the conversation is really about the easiest way to teach literacy. Of course, people have to be convinced so they understand."

Mar'ia Nikolavna, biting her lips and knitting her brows, stood at the table opposite Riazanov and unconsciously followed the

---

5. This is a pun in Russian: *shkola* (school) and *shkura* (skin or hide).

movement of his hands with her eyes: he slowly but firmly rolled one book into a tube.

"How can it be," she asked. "Does that mean it's all untrue?" Her face suddenly flushed.

"What's untrue?"

"In general, everything that's been published?"

Riazanov smiled.

"Why are you smiling? Tell me. Is it all untrue? Then, at least, I'll know."

"No, some things are true, but it's only that. . . ."

"Only what?"

"You have to know how to read."

"Why do people write so that you have to rack your brains over it?"

"What can be done? They've got that habit."

"Do you also write like this?"

"Yes, I do. What sort of writer would I be if dragged in everything that came into my head? That's the way the world's organized," said Riazanov, forming some little cutouts from the paper, "so that when a person's stomach aches, it's customary to refrain from talking about it: it's not proper. What's the big deal? It's the most natural thing, yet it's not proper to talk about the suffering of one's abdominal organs, so that's that. Social norms require that in this case the patient not announce his illness in public. If one's head hurts, one can say so; if your foot aches, you can say so; if your side hurts—even in the presence of important people, you can say so; but if one's stomach aches—impossible: they'll eject you immediately. That's how it is! There's nothing you can do: social norms demand that when your stomach hurts, you nonchalantly give yourself over to various pursuits and to paying compliments; if you can't, well, stay home and say you're having an attack of nerves."

"That's so absurd!"

"You think so? No, ma'am, not at all. Social norms are not so foolish as it may seem. They're based on the profound study of human nature; and this nature is such that if you allow a person to talk about his bellyache, then the only thing he'll talk about is his gut. There's nothing good about that, you'll have to agree! The main thing is that the matter won't end there; debates will ensue—how, from what, why does his stomach hurt? What did you do or what did you eat? Did you overeat? Did you strain yourself? What did you try to lift? Who made you do it? Why didn't you call someone else and order him to do it? 'I would have been glad to, but he doesn't obey.' 'Why doesn't he?' 'He doesn't have any money.' 'Why doesn't he?' 'He's poor.' 'As a result of what? Why isn't another person poor?' You wind up in such a thicket you can't find your way out."

Mar'ia Nikolavna pondered this and as she was standing near the table, she remained there motionless with the books in her hands. At last she sighed, put the books down on the table, and said, as if talking to herself: "Why didn't I ever think about this before?" Then she added, "Listen, these norms are really appalling."

"How so? Their goal is to eliminate any unpleasant, tiresome conversations and to make our life an easy and pleasant pursuit."

"That's not what I want at all," Mar'ia Nikolavna said passionately.

"Ah! Well, that's a different matter. So then, you declare, it's not what you want."

Mar'ia Nikolavna knitted her brows. "You seem to be making fun of me?"

"Why are you talking such nonsense?"

"I won't talk nonsense."

"Then I won't make fun of you."

She smiled and began turning the pages of the issue of *Notes of the Fatherland* lying on the table.

"Tell me, please," she began, putting her hand on the book. "What do you see here?"

"In these books?" asked Riazanov. After a little thought, he replied, "I see the battle on the Field of Kulikovo, and I hear the clash of swords, the neighing of horses, and the groans of those dying.[6] 'At times the Tatars dominate the Russians, at times the Russian dominate the Tatars.'[7] And even more than that, I see the feats of civilian stupidity, characteristic of docile Russians."

"And after this, can you yourself write?"

"Why not?"

"After what you've said?"

"It's possible even after this; if none of this had happened, there'd be no reason to write."

She stood there in silence for a few minutes, then suddenly said cheerfully, pointing to the piles of books lying on the floor: "Well, let's pick up all these dead tomes!"

"We can."

They both set about putting the books into the cupboard.

Just then Shchetinin came in.

"What are you doing?"

"Celebrating a funeral feast for the departed," replied Riazanov, leaning over the books.

"I see! While I can't cope with the ones still alive!" he said, opening the desk.

"It's more difficult, the living," said Riazanov.

"Its simply a misfortune. The peasants asked for leave to go into town for the fair, but the next day they were nowhere to be found. The steward sent one fine fellow to make purchases . . . well, that steward's also a nice man! He knew that the fellow liked to drink, but he gave him some money. He's just returned, drunk as a skunk; of course, he's back without the money and without the purchases. The devil only knows what he did there. Go try to find out from him: he's so drunk, he can't even talk straight. What

6. The location of the famous battle fought between the armies of the Golden Horde and various Russian principalities under the united command of Prince Dmitrii of Moscow in 1380. It is widely regarded as the turning point when Mongol influence began to wane and Muscovite power to rise.

7. Source unknown.

a disgusting situation," said Shchetinin, rummaging around the table.

"Well, so what's to be done now?" asked Riazanov.

"Yes! What indeed? No, you tell me, what's to be done? You always say that. . . ."

"What do I say?"

"That . . . there's no need to hold them accountable, and that's that."

"*And that's that*; let's suppose I could say that. But when did I say there was no need to hold them accountable?"

"Well, yes, of course," replied Shchetinin unwillingly.

"When was it?"

"What do you mean, when? In general. . . ."

"No, listen, tell me, please, why do you make false statements saying *in general*? Here, my friend, there's a witness: Mar'ia Nikolavna in person."

"And what a witness she is," replied Shchetinin, half joking.

Mar'ia Nikolavna, who was still arranging books, suddenly glanced around, lowered her hand, and stared directly at her husband; but without saying anything, she returned to picking up her books. Shchetinin didn't notice her expression, but turned around on his chair to face Riazanov and said: "No, tell me, as a matter of fact, what should I do, how should I act?"

"With that fine fellow?"

"Yes, with him. We trusted him with the money, and he spent it all on drink."

"I told you once before what to do, didn't I?"

"You said turn to the district police . . . that's what!"

"Well, so then? Consequently, do you consider legal retribution unsatisfactory?"

"I do."

"Well, then you come up with something else. Why ask me?"

"I want to know your opinion."

"You don't need it for anything. The point is, how to take revenge on a man for a personal insult; so then why do you need advice from an outsider? You trusted him; he didn't merit your trust;

you're the offended party, not me. I don't have any feelings about him. Even if he drank you all up, and your entire estate, with all its farmlands and wastelands—what's that to me?"

"Put yourself in my place!"

"I don't want to imagine it. Why should I? I'll never be in that position, and even if this could ever happen, how do I know how I might act then? Perhaps I'd impale this fine fellow, or perhaps I'd limit myself to knocking out only two of his teeth, or perhaps I'd give him a reward of a hundred rubles for what he did."

"No, that's not right. Just imagine they'd behaved like that with you right now."

"I don't understand why these imaginings are necessary—they don't explain a thing. Just imagine that right at this moment someone smeared you over completely with honey! What would you do? Imagine that they'd run over you with a wheel. Imagine as much as you like: what can come of that?"

"There's only one thing I can't understand," Shchetinin said in the meantime, not listening and addressing no one in particular.

"What can't you understand?" asked Riazanov.

"I don't understand why it can't be stated in a straightforward manner. If he'd said to me: 'I'm going to the fair; I want to get drunk.' Without saying a word, I'd have given him a silver ruble—'Go ahead, old man!' Why not, it's a holiday; I understand; he's worked all year, toiled away—why shouldn't he drink and have a good time at the fair? Is it a crime? I ask only one thing: be straightforward! No, don't you see, deception's better. 'For pity's sake,' he says, 'now I've sworn it off and won't ever take another drop.' You'll agree, it's despicable!"

"What is, swearing it off?"

"No, deceiving."

"I agree that in general, in principle, it's despicable to deceive."

"Well, then. That's all I'm talking about. Be straightforward!"

"Yes. I'm going to peek at your cards—that doesn't matter; but don't you peek at mine—that's despicable. But maybe I won't even peek: just tell me frankly what cards you have. That's splendid."

"That's not it at all. If you play, then in my opinion, you should play honorably."

"I don't know why you use such words. 'Honorably!' The enemy always acts in a despicable manner: the more despicable it is, the more honor he attains."

"Oh, no, my friend. I don't want to abide by such rules."

"With rules like that they should make you a commanding officer. Very interesting! Would you, for example, issue the following order to your army: attack the enemy camp at night? Isn't that despicable? To attack when they're all asleep? Therefore, you have to send an adjutant to say: 'Hey, you, watch out! Tonight we intend to overwhelm you; so be on guard; keep your wits about you!'"

Shchetinin made no reply.

"Or perhaps you wish to imitate Aristides and defeat your enemies with generosity?[8] You can do that."

"So what? Yes, I want to do it."

"Yes. Of course, on the one hand, it is noble, there's no doubt about it; but in domestic affairs, I venture, it's not profitable."

"That's my affair."

"Of course. Vanquish them from the side as much as you like. Nobody will prevent you. But to count on the enemy's generosity— that, my friend, in my opinion, is a risky thing to do."

"I'm not counting on anyone or anything besides myself," Shchetinin said with a disgruntled look and once more started rifling through some papers.

"So then what are you going on about?"

"Nothing," he replied abruptly; but after a few moments he reconsidered, locked his desk, stretched, and said with a yawn: "So, therefore, in your opinion, it's an act of war that Fed'ka Skvortsov spent three rubles on drink?"

"Yes."

---

8. Aristides (530–468 BCE) was an ancient Athenian general and statesman, nicknamed "the Just." The ancient historian Herodotus cited him as "the best and most honorable man in Athens."

"And that the Kriukov peasants steal wood from me—is that also an act of war?"

"It is."

"Hmm. A fine war, I'll say!"

"A partisan war, my friend, partisan. Mostly they attack suddenly, helter-skelter, each in his own way: here, Fed'ka Skvortsov, there, the countrywoman Vasilisa strikes with her metal poker, while the Kriukov peasants...."

"They're all partisans?"

"They are."

"And in your opinion wherever there're scoundrels, there'll be a war? Is that what you're trying to say?"

"Not exactly."

"Well, then what?"

"Here's what: wherever there are strong and weak, rich and poor, master and worker—there's also war; what sort of war it is, whether it's correct or incorrect, is not our business to decide."

Shchetinin fell silent once again.

"This much, my friend, even Ivan Stepanych knows," continued Riazanov. "A few days ago he said to me, 'I'll be damned,' he says. 'In the *Moscow News* I read there're wars going on all over the world. Why,' he says, 'in Persia, an uncivilized state, even there,' he says, 'the women are rebelling.'"

Shchetinin smiled unintentionally; after some thought, he remarked: "That means, in your opinion, there's no reason to wish for better servants. Is that what you're saying?"

"Why? It's permissible to desire anything. You can wish for anything you want."

"But you think this desire is unreasonable."

"No. I think merely it's a little unusual. It's just as if, for example, I wished that a *good* blister would suddenly erupt on your face or that you would be overcome by a *good* fever. You have to agree, that would be a very unusual desire. Isn't that right?"

Riazanov kept lifting books from the floor and handing them to Mar'ia Nikolavna. Shchetinin sat with his back to his desk, reclining in his armchair with his hands clasped behind his neck; some sort of awkward, strained smile flitted across his face; for a long time he cast his eyes silently around the room, as if considering something; at last he cleared his throat and began speaking, dragging out his words: "You keep saying—this isn't right and that isn't. . . ."

"Yes," Riazanov said, leaning over a book.

"Meanwhile, you've been here almost a month; have you given me at least one bit of useful, practical advice, or said something from which I could draw some direct, genuine benefit? Huh? Can you recall a time?"

Riazanov picked up a pile of books; holding them in his hands, he replied: "Yes. If you invited me here so you could confer with me about your estate, then I congratulate you." Having said this, he handed Mar'ia Nikolavna the last books from the floor and wiped his hands with his handkerchief.

"Well, not for that, of course," Shchetinin began quickly. "You yourself know that very well. No, but I thought that in general your opinions would have more . . . practical foundations."

"You were mistaken. Pity!"

"No, not that at all. I've known for a long time that you and I don't agree about some things; but it was exactly this difference in our views that I was counting on. I thought that by expressing your convictions you'd help me clarify my own."

"Hmm," muttered Riazanov.

"Yes," Shchetinin said, hastily interrupting him. "The proverb is well known: '*Du choc des opinions jaillit la vérité.*'"[9]

"What did you say?"

"I said, '*Du choc des opinions jaillit la vérité.*'"

"Isn't it that '*plenus venter non student libenter?*'"[10]

"No, it isn't."

"Not that! Well, so then what?"

---

9. "Disputation is the sifter out of truth" (Fr.). The original of the proverb has been traced back to works of the French writer C. P. Colardeau (1732–1766).

10. "A full stomach does not like to study" (Lat.). A Roman proverb.

"No, don't you see," continued Shchetinin, without listening, "it happens all by itself. I say you object: thus two opinions are in conflict. You must agree that only when two conflicting opinions do battle will sense emerge: light and darkness, good and evil, plus and minus. . . ."

"It adds up to minus, my friend, minus."

"Yes! Well, the hell with it! But it doesn't matter; the point isn't in a comparison."

"Of course. Good practitioners always make bad theorists."

Mar'ia Nikolavna smiled and sat down.

"Yes. So, as I was saying," Shchetinin continued in a somewhat dissatisfied tone of voice, "it's only necessary for the debaters to respect each other's opinions."

"What for?"

"What do you mean by 'What for'? If we don't respect each other's opinions, then what will happen?"

"An argument."

"No, I think there'll be a fight."

"I think so, too."

"So then, in that verbal fight will the one who defeats the other be right?"

"Yes, indeed. Of course. There are no other kinds of arguments."

"No, my friend; I don't approve of such arguments."

"Then you must like the kind of arguments when both people are right."

"No. In my opinion if one argues, then one does so without insulting the other person."

"That's a commendable rule. No question about it. But I still don't understand why you went through this long rigmarole."

"And I want to say that in general I've been noticing some bitterness lately in everyone, in absolutely everyone."

"You didn't notice it before? So, in other words, you've become disillusioned not only with me, but with other people. Is that so?"

"No; don't you see, I'm an easygoing man, I like people, but I can't, I simply can't regard them as enemies against whom one must constantly take precautions, always expect intrigues. . . . I can't abide that. Well, what do you want? There, I simply can't, and that's that."

After saying this, Shchetinin didn't look at anyone and scraped the desk with his penknife.

"Yes. Well, they say," said Riazanov, "that it was good to live in the days of King Solomon: each man sat under his own tent and in his own vineyard while King Solomon sat on his throne and judged them all. There were no arguments and no fights in those days."

"To tell you the truth, so help me God, it was better in those days than now," said Shchetinin.

"Who's to blame, my dear friend, that with such peace-loving inclinations you're compelled to live at such a hostile time? What can you do? Honestly, I don't know."

"I do know, my friend," said Shchetinin, getting up.

"Well, if you do, there's nothing to talk about," said Riazanov, also standing up, and he left the room.

Shchetinin stood for a while near the window, whistled, then put his hands in his pockets; staring at his feet, he walked slowly toward the door.

"Listen," said Mar'ia Nikolavna.

"What is it?" Shchetinin paused in the doorway without turning around.

"What language did he use when he answered you then?"

"Latin."

"What does it mean?"

"Some nonsense." Shchetinin took a step forward.

"No, it's not nonsense," she said after him.

Shchetinin was about to pause for a moment, but reconsidered and left the room with a measured pace.

CHAPTER IX

———

IT WAS THE WARMEST TIME OF YEAR: THE MOWING HAD begun and the rye was turning brown; a stifling, suffocating breeze was drifting lazily across the lakes, barely stirring the tops of the reeds. Then suddenly it would begin to whirl, rising up like a black column and racing through the meadows. The sky remained blue and cloudless; at night there were occasional thunderstorms.

Of late Shchetinin had begun working even more than before. He spent entire days at the farm or in the forest; for the most part he would come home late in the evening tired and worn out; he would consume a large quantity of sour clotted milk and go to bed.[1] All arguments with Riazanov ceased completely. This occurred suddenly, as if by mutual consent: both of them stopped arguing at one and the same time, and that was that. More and more their conversations were reduced to the simple exchange of information, objections were limited to offhand remarks of the sort that—yes, of course, naturally; well, it, I tell you, however . . . of course, and

---

1   *Prostokvasha.*

so forth. Sometimes it happened that Shchetinin would get carried away telling some story and Riazanov would listen in silence while staring at the tablecloth; after hearing him out, he would still keep silent. Shchetinin couldn't refrain and would ask: "Why don't you say anything? Don't you think I know what you're thinking?"

"So much the better for you and the nicer for me," Riazanov would reply and then he himself would begin telling Mar'ia Nikolavna how, for example, he and Shchetinin, during the time they both spent at the university, had learned to march.

"It was a splendid time," Riazanov said. "Lectures would finish, you'd be sick and tired of hearing about Roman law, collect your notebooks, and head to the riding academy. The main thing is, it was located nearby, and that was good. The inspector used to say only one thing: 'Don't lean back, gentlemen, for heaven's sake! Do me a favor, push your chest forward!' Well, and off you go."

Riazanov continued, "I remember one fellow who was particularly skilled. His name was Troitsky: he was a seminary student, already about thirty years old; he'd come all the way from Orenburg on foot to study,[2] and took up history; now he's a professor. Well then, what a torment it would be; he wasn't able to turn around to the left, no matter what he did. He was an enormous man, round-shouldered, with long arms. The inspector would badger him: 'Mr. Troitsky, stand up straight! You, non-commissioned officer, correct Mr. Troitsky! Can you feel your comrade's elbow?' 'I do, sir, Fëdor Fëdorovich, sir, I do, sir,' and he'd even grind his teeth."

"And did you also learn to march?" asked Mar'ia Nikolavna, staring at Riazanov with particular curiosity.

"Yes, I did, too, and 'Eyes right!' I did just as I was supposed to. Of course."

"Well, how come?" Mar'ia Nikolavna said with a dissatisfied look. "Why did you do it?"

---

2. Orenburg is a transcontinental city and administrative center located on the Ural River some 900 miles southeast of Moscow, close to the border with Kazakhstan.

"After all, am I worse than any of the others?"

But Mar'ia Nikolavna didn't get much satisfaction from these stories; each time she was left alone with Riazanov, she tried to draw him into more serious conversation; besides, she borrowed books from him and read them one after another without interruption. Strolling around her garden, she would approach his window and invite him to join her. Sometimes they went far into the fields and wandered along the riverbanks. She would interrogate him about what had happened previously, what was going on now, and would listen to his tales avidly; as she listened, her face became more serious and intense; at times she even wept, but then she quickly wiped away her tears and began fanning her face with her handkerchief. After one such conversation she asked Riazanov: "Listen, is it really true he knows nothing about all this?"

"How could he not know?"

"Then why hasn't he ever said anything about it to me?"

"I don't know."

"I'll never, never forgive him," she said, rolling her eyes angrily.

The domestic household proceeded of its own accord—she hardly got involved with it. Shchetinin seemed not to notice these walks of theirs; only once did he ask his wife: "And what about your school?"

"I've postponed it until autumn," Mar'ia Nikolavna replied. "It's summer now: who wants to study? It's too hot."

Shchetinin looked her straight in the eye, but made no reply and began singing. She started talking about something else.

"Why have you stopped arguing with Aleksandr Vasil'ich?" she asked Riazanov.

"You saw how unpleasant he found it."

"So what?"

"Why should I irritate the man for no good reason?"

"Yes, that's true. Well, at least you could argue with me! I really like it when you argue."

However, Mar'ia Nikolavna couldn't restrain herself and sometimes in her husband's presence she would begin some conversation that had the potential for eliciting passionate debate; in such situations Riazanov usually put an end to the incipient argument at the very start with some brief observation to which it was impossible to object.

One evening he was sitting in his room and planning to go out for a walk; suddenly Mar'ia Nikolavna came in. "Come see us at once!"

"What for?"

"Guests have arrived, including a young lady. I'd very much like you to meet her."

"Why is that necessary?"

"It's not necessary at all, it's just that. . . . Well, I'm imploring you."

Riazanov shrugged his shoulders.

"Do come!"

Mar'ia Nikolavna hoisted up her skirt and hurried back to the house.

Riazanov found the guests on the terrace: Mar'ia Nikolavna was pouring tea; next to her sat a lady about thirty-five years old; she had a thin face and slightly squinting eyes that she was trying to make appear piercing. There, too, a little removed, stood the mediator, Semën Semënych, with whom Riazanov was acquainted; he was chatting with the lady's husband. Mar'ia Nikolavna smiled and introduced Riazanov to the guests. He sat down at the table. The newly arrived lady squinted all the more, but when she encountered Riazanov's eyes, she blinked and began to rub her eye. At the same time the mediator was saying to her husband: "What then would you have me do? The devil must have urged them on—they set fires three years in a row. They set fires, and that's that. What can I get from them?"

"Isn't it possible to get anything from them?" the landowner persisted. "Put yourself in my position: I have to send my wife abroad. Could you perhaps resettle them?"

"How many times have you resettled them already?"

"So what? Well, twice before. What difference does it make?"

"Well, how can you want to do that? It's inhumane. If you re-settle them for a third time, they'll go begging."

"I don't really intend to go through with it, but might it be possible at least to threaten them with resettlement?"

"Let's have tea," Mar'ia Nikolavna summoned them.

"No, wait, I'll tell you, Mar'ia Nikolavna," said the mediator, picking up a glass. "*Merci*, I take it without cream. I inherited a small estate as part of my property—the village Otrada—do you know it? Two thousand rubles in arrears; they're not paying for the third year in a row. Just think of that! My predecessor, Pavel Ivanych, tried and tried, and then gave up: he couldn't do a thing. He brought in the military, thrashed them—but to no avail. But in three weeks I recovered all of it, to the last kopeck, and didn't have to lay a hand on anyone."

"How did you do it?" asked Mar'ia Nikolavna.

"Very simply: I went out and called them all together: 'Money!' No money, and that was that. The common people are robbers. So, no money? No. All right. Well, immediately, the first one I saw in the crowd, I said, 'Bring him over here!' 'You don't want to pay up?' 'No.' 'Seize him!' To the next one I said, 'You don't want to pay either?' 'Sir, dear father!' 'Don't say a thing! Seize him!' And in that way I selected ten men and locked them up in the barn with only bread and water to eat! It was work time, you know, and for a peasant every hour's valuable—so sit there! I said to the village elder: 'You're responsible for them. If you release even one of those scoundrels, I'll send all your sons off to the army![3] That'll be the last time you see them. Splendid.' Then I left. I came back in a week, 'Well, lads, how're things?' 'Dear father, provider, have mercy!' 'Aha! Have you repented? Well?' 'Have us punished!' 'No, why on earth? I won't punish you, but now you can all leave and go home to your village, and ask your buddies to help you out!' I released them— half an hour later they came back and brought seven hundred sil-

---

3. The term of military service in eighteenth-century Russia was for life. In 1793 it was reduced to twenty-five years. In 1834 it was reduced to twenty years plus five years in reserve and in 1855 to twelve years plus three years of reserve.

ver rubles. Splendid. Then I locked them up for another week! I can tell you what happened: they grew thin as rails and their eyes were sunken. I returned—it was the same thing all over again. In three weeks I'd managed to recover the whole amount to the last kopeck."

After finishing his story, the mediator took a gulp of tea from his glass and glanced at everyone with a satisfied look.

"Yes," said the landowner with a sigh. "Well, Semën Semënych, you do it for others, but not for me. That's not good, sir."

"Allow me to observe," began the mediator, growing animated, "what a strange fellow you are. How can you compare your men with these? You can lock up your peasants for as long as you like. Nothing will come of it: they'll merely die of starvation. What can you get out of them? After all, they're as poor as beggars."

"No; what of it, sir? That's no excuse. It's that you have no desire to do anything about it. That's the main thing."

"You're quite a character, excuse me for saying so," shouted the mediator.

An argument ensued and continued while they drank their tea. Riazanov was silent the whole time. After tea the priest arrived and asked: "Where's the master?"

"At the farm."

"As usual."

Mar'ia Nikolavna called Riazanov out into the hall and said to him: "Please talk with this lady; I'd really like to know your opinion of her."

"But I don't know how to converse with ladies."

"Never mind. Then how do you talk to me? Am I not a lady too?" she said with a laugh. "You know, as a matter of fact," she added, "if you only knew how all of them have begun to appall me! But there's nothing to be done; I have to go back. Come along," she whispered to him, going out onto the terrace and turning to him with a smile. Then she took her guest by the arm, went out into the garden, and called Riazanov over. The three of them strolled along the tree-lined lane. It started to grow dark.

"Are you a writer?" the lady asked Riazanov.

"I am."

"Ah, please describe the local district."

"What for?"

"You can't imagine the sort of atrocities being committed here, especially at court."

Riazanov was silent.

"*Vous n'avez-pas l'idée, ma chère, ce qui c'est,*" she said, turning to Mar'ia Nikolavna.[4] "It's just terrible! Just imagine, for half a year they won't give my husband a certificate. Please, expose all this, Monsieur Riazanov! I beg of you."

"We'll be getting new courts soon," remarked Mar'ia Nikolavna.[5]

"*Je vous en félicite,*" replied the lady.[6] "No, spare me! We know these new courts. It's always like that. Before everyone was shouting: 'Ah, mediators, mediators!' So, we got our mediators. What use are they, *je vous demande un peu*?[7] They can't recover the arrears! New courts! *Non, ma chère, on ne nous y prendra plus.*"[8]

They got to the end of the lane in silence and then turned back toward the house.

"And then they came up with some kind of *zemstvo*," the lady was about to begin again. "Katkov's telling the truth,[9] *que c'est une kyrielle. C'est bien vrai, ma chère.*[10] I don't know what it is. No one has any money, *les chemins sont atroces. . . .*"[11]

"Would you care to rest a bit?" Mar'ia Nikolavna interrupted her as they started up the stairs.

---

4. "You have no idea, my dear, what's happening." (Fr.)

5. As mandated by Alexander II's judicial reform of 1864.

6. "I congratulate you." (Fr.)

7. "I ask you." (Fr.)

8. "No, my dear, you can't deceive us any more." (Fr.)

9. M. N. Katkov (1818–1887), the editor of *Moscow News,* came out in opposition to the judicial reforms.

10. "It's no more than a big waste of time. It's really true, my dear." (Fr.)

11. "The roads are terrible." (Fr.)

"No, sir. There was also a case in Penza,"[12] the priest began when he saw Riazanov. "A man of the cloth was walking along the street; on the other side some drunken tradesman happened by: 'Hey, hey, hey! Ho, ho, ho!' he says. . . ."

The priest stood up from the table, placed one hand on his side and imitated the tradesman.

"No, sir, what do you think? For doing this, they exiled that . . . fellow. And the only thing he did was say 'Ho, ho, ho.' That's how it is, sir," the priest concluded, casting a sarcastic glance at Riazanov.

"That's really something," said the mediator. "I had an incident in Saratov.[13] I really managed to stop one young man!"

Riazanov went out into the hall.

"Listen! No, please get away from here! I can't stand seeing them together with you."

"Yes, I wanted to leave."

"I'm so annoyed; it's revolting. Forgive me for inviting you!"

Riazanov returned to the annex and got ready to go to bed. The mediator arrived back around midnight. They had prepared a bed for him in the office.

"I have a little proposal to make to you," he said, going in to see Riazanov.

"What is it?"

"Would you care to travel around the district with me tomorrow? It might be of interest to you as a resident of the capital."

Riazanov thought about it and agreed to go.

---

12. Penza is a city and administrative center located on the Sura River, almost 400 miles southeast of Moscow.

13. Saratov is a city, administrative center, and major port on the Volga River.

CHAPTER X

———

THE STEWARD WOKE RIAZANOV AND THE MEDIATOR at four in the morning. They went out onto the porch: the sky was overcast, cocks were crowing, and it looked as if it would soon start raining; the carriage stood next to the porch. The mediator yawned and sighed.

"Why in the world would you do this? You could've slept," grumbled Ivan Stepanych, wearing only a shirt as he glanced out of the window.

"Impossible, sir—it's my work," replied the mediator.

They got into the carriage and set off.

People from the village were preparing to head off to the field; sleepy women carried buckets; there were sheep and an acrid smell of fresh smoke; peasant men doffed their caps.

"Hello," the mediator shouted to them in a drowsy voice and then dozed off.

They came into a field: there is dew, a light breeze, and the sky is turning red in the east; a quail takes flight above the brown winter crops. . . .

———

The ravine is overgrown with hazel trees; there is a bridge below. The trace horses, lowering their heads, proceed downward and then start up again as one. Suddenly there's a strong jolt; the mediator snorts, opens his eyes, looks aimlessly from side to side, and then dozes off again.

The fog is lifting and the distance is becoming clearer and clearer, the colors get brighter, the air, more transparent, and one after another distant villages appear, as well as forests and lakes. . . . Suddenly the dew begins glistening, the brass on the shaft horse's neck lights up, and the horses' long dark shadows race across the grass—the sun has risen.

Riazanov looked and looked: he observed how the horses are running, how the larks are diving from above into the fresh rye and once again, as if climbing steps, rising higher and higher; how the herd is grazing on the hillside. . . . A pig carcass is lying in the hollow and a crow is sitting on top of it.

"Semën Semënych! Hey, Semën Semënych!"

"Mmm?"

"Time to wake up!"

"Hmm."

"Semën Semënych!"

"Mmm?"

"We've arrived."

"Ah. We've arrived. Where's the foreman?"

"I'm here, Semën Semënych. I'll help you out."

"You have a samovar?"

"It'll be ready soon."

"Hurry up! Well, how are things?" asks the mediator, entering the district office.

"All's well, thank heaven, sir," the foreman replies with a bow.

The clerk, wearing a nankeen jacket, wipes dust off the table with his sleeve, bows, and retreats to the wall.

"All right," says the mediator, taking a seat and examining the walls with his still sleepy eyes. His face is haggard and there's a red scar on his forehead.

The foreman stands there, leaning forward a little, clasping his hands behind his back.

"Bring in the briefcase!"

The foreman and the clerk rush out of the hut.

The sun is starting to heat up intensely, flies are knocking against the window, and the horses are being unharnessed in the courtyard.

"This foreman I have is not bad at all," says the mediator to Riazanov. "But he's a bit inexperienced and not too nimble."

"Mmm," replies Riazanov.

The foreman brings in the briefcase carefully, as if afraid to spill something; placing it on the table, he withdraws. The clerk retreats to the cupboard on tiptoes and stands at attention behind the foreman's back.

"Well, and how are the arrears going?" asks the mediator, placing the chain of office around his neck.

"Not well, sir," replies the foreman with a sigh.

"Why aren't you coercing them, my good man?" asks the mediator.

"We are, sir," replies the clerk in a low voice, looking blankly at the mediator.

"We are, sir," the foreman repeats, leaning his head glumly to one side.

"You must be doing a bad job of it," says the mediator. "A landowner was complaining to me that so far you've been unable to pay the remaining five hundred rubles due from last year, from October. That's a disgrace!"

The clerk approaches the table swiftly; digging through the documents, he points respectfully with his little finger to the book, saying: "From the fifteenth of February of the current year there remain 495 rubles and 72 kopecks owed, sir."

"Well, yes," confirms the mediator. "You're weak, my friend, that's what I can tell you," he said, addressing the foreman.

The foreman sighs.

"Do you really think I enjoy hearing complaints about you?"

The foreman wrinkles his brows and tries not to look at the mediator.

"Well, you can seize their property and sell it. Where's the good news? Judge for yourself!"

"There's little good news, sir," replies the foreman, staring at his boots.

"That's the whole point," the mediator concludes didactically. "You're not watching your step."

There were several moments of awkward silence.

"Oh, oh, oh!" sighed the mediator. "Well then, my friend?"

"Yes, sir?" asks the foreman hesitantly.

"What about that samovar?"

"It's ready, sir."

The clerk rushes to the door.

"Hmm, yes," says the mediator, staring thoughtfully at the ceiling.

"It's all in God's hands, sir," remarks the foreman.

"Yes, my friend, once they sell your property, you'll learn God's will."

The clerk could be heard fanning the samovar in the entrance hall.

"Do you have any items to discuss?" asks the mediator suddenly.

The foreman looks at the clerk in the doorway and motions to him with his finger.

"Yes, yar'exlency," says the clerk, coming into the room and brushing himself off. "There's a complaint from the temporarily obligated peasant woman Vikulina from the village of Zavidovka, about a beating she received from a drunken peasant from the same village, one Fëdor Ignat'ev."[1]

"Has it been investigated?"

"Yes, sir," replies the foreman gleefully.

"How was it resolved?"

"To give them both a little scare, sir."

"How?"

"With some dry branches, sir," replies the foreman, now laughing openly.

---

1. A peasant who after emancipation in 1861 was obligated to pay quit-rent (in place of labor) for use of the land.

"Ah. That's good. The main thing is: I don't want any drunkenness. You hear?"

"Yes, sir."

"Anything else?"

"Yes, sir," the clerk reports, stepping forward. "There's still the matter of the pursuit of two pigs and their piglets belonging to the peasant Pëtr Gerasimov of the district department."

"Who chased them?"

"A local resident, sir. Pëtr Gerasimov's now complaining that since, he says, during the time of the chase, he says, his boy was beaten. . . ."

"Well!"

"But the local resident in his statement maintains that it was limited to pulling his forelock, sir."

"Yes. So how does the matter stand now?"

"Well, Semën Semënych, as far as that's concerned, they question even more," the foreman intervenes, "whether, he says, these same pigs were chased at all. . . ."

"Yes. . . ."

"That is, wrongly, sir," adds the clerk.

"Exactly," confirms the foreman. "Why this confusion occurred, well, apparently. . . ."

"This hostility of theirs goes way back, sir," remarks the clerk mysteriously. "And, in fact, it concerns women, sir."

"Indeed it does! To put it straight, they made such a mountain out of molehill, a real mountain. . . . Ah, is the samovar ready?"

The foreman rushes into the entrance hall and brings back the samovar; the clerk hands around cups and some pretzels.

"How did you resolve this matter?" asks the mediator.

"We haven't been able to," replies the foreman, shooing some flies out of the teapot. "Get out, damn you! I have to say they'd like to bring it to your attention. . . ."

"A reprimand was issued so as not to trouble you with such trifles," adds the clerk.

"You must fine them," the mediator decides. "Fine them one silver ruble each for the benefit of the church! You hear?"

"Yes, sir."

The mediator brews tea; Riazanov reads the announcements and rosters of local officials displayed on the walls.

"The main thing is," continues the mediator, "alcohol. I don't want to catch a whiff of it ever again! You hear?"

"Yes, sir," the foreman replies reluctantly.

"All evil comes from it," the mediator argues.

"That's true, sir," the foreman agrees.

The clerk coughs unobtrusively into his fist.

"A drunk's capable of anything. He'll even box your ears. . . ."

"He will. That's for sure."

"And he'll set fires."

"He will, sir. He certainly can."

"Just look at all the fires!"

"Yes, yes. Good Lord!"

"The common people say the Poles are setting the fires. . . ."

"Exactly, they do. Ah, the rascals!"

"No, it's not them."

"Not them at all. Why would they?"

"It's all the fault of alcohol."

"Yes, indeed. It's all from that damned alcohol. There's something I wanted to ask you, Semën Semënych."

"What?"

"What about the quitrent we pay the landowner now. . . ."

"Well?"

"People say, what difference does it make, they say; it doesn't matter how much we pay, nothing will come of it."

"Yes. Until they pay the redemption fee, it'll do no good. They'll pay all their life, but the land will still belong to the landowner."

"So that's what! In other words, his reign will know no end?"[2]

"Exactly. What can be done? You're all stupid."

"That's fair to say. Fools! What fools we are!"

---

2. A reference to Luke 1:33: "And He shall reign over the house of Jacob for ever; and of His kingdom there shall be no end."

"Precisely, lads. How many times have I told you?" the mediator says with a sigh. "Do you have any cream?"

"Yes, sir."

The foreman brings in a wooden cup with cream and fishes
some flies out of it.

"Oh, damn them! If you please, Semën Semënych!"

"So, you must also have a lot of flies?"

"Yes, indeed—what a misfortune," the foreman replies, smiling deferentially. "Where do they all come from?"

The mediator and Riazanov drink their tea; the foreman looks
out the window; the clerk, having nothing else to do, arranges the
papers, pens, and seals lying on the desk.

Silence.

"Well, and how's the school faring?" asks the mediator, sipping
tea from his glass.

"Well, thank God."

"Is the priest teaching?"

"At times he does. No problem."

"Are there many pupils?"

"Enough."

"How many exactly?"

"Well, I have to say," the foreman looks questioningly at the
clerk. "Must be about five."

"In general, very few, sir," replies the clerk.

"Really not very many, sir," the foreman reports with a nod of
his head.

"You should take care," says the mediator, "that they come to
study. It'll be of value to you all."

"That's clear, sir. A lad who knows how to read these days can,
for example, pick up any book and read it. It's very nice, sir."

"Yes, and if more of them were literate, there'd be less drunkenness. Instead of going to the tavern, they'd stay home and read a book."

"A book. They'd stay home and read a book. That's true, sir."

"Why is it so few want to go to school?"

"Because, I suppose, it's due to stupidity, sir."

"Well, it's your job to encourage them, explain it to them."

"I've already encouraged them and said to the priest: 'You,' I said, 'father, take care; the mediator ordered it so we don't have to take the blame for it.'"

"What did he say?"

"Well, 'All right,' he says, 'go on! My hay,' he says, 'is still not cut.' That's what. Besides, peasants are afraid that those who can read and write will all be sent off to become *cantonists*."[3]

"That's pure nonsense! Don't you believe that!"

"Yes, sir!"

"And what happened to that paper I sent a few days ago—was it signed?"

"I doubt that, sir."

"What? You doubt that? What sort of a foreman are you, anyway? I'll be back here in about three days, and I want that paper signed by then. Understand?"

"Yes, sir," the foreman replied hesitantly.

The mediator was starting to perspire and was wiping his face with his handkerchief.

"I forgot to inform you, sir, that the priest's come with the gardener. They have some small matters to discuss."

"What matters?"

"Concerning the calves. The priest's calves wandered into the gardener's vegetable patch; the gardener rounded them up and drove them into his courtyard, and locked them up. The priest came at once; on and on he went: 'How dare you round up the colonel's calves?'"

"The colonel's calves?"

"That's to say, the priest's calves. He thinks that he's a colonel."

"Yes."

"Well, so his mother-in-law butts in and the calves are taken away. . . ."

"Then what?"

---

3. Cantonists were underage sons of Russian conscripts who from 1721 were educated in special canton schools for future military service.

"Who can sort it out? The gardener's complaining: he says the calves trampled six silver rubles' worth of vegetables, and the priest's now demanding fifteen rubles from him for the humiliation, or he'll. . . ."

"Fifteen silver rubles," confirms the clerk.

"What humiliation?"

"The insult to his mother-in-law."

"How did he insult her?"

"He called her a slobberer. God knows what. 'You're a slobberer,' he says," the foreman explains with a laugh. "Well, the priest says to me, he says that's very offensive. And now he's demanding fifteen silver rubles from him."

The mediator also starts laughing; even the clerk is giggling into his fist.

"Well, I'll sort this out later," says the mediator, standing up. "For now, my friend, here's what: have the horses brought round!"

"They're ready, sir."

"Good man," says the mediator, patting the foreman on the shoulder.

The foreman bows, then together with the clerk escorts the mediator onto the porch.

A peasant is sitting on the coachman's seat; the horses belong to the militia.

"You know the road?"

"Rest assured."

"Watch out, my man," the foreman says to the peasant. "Take it easy, so nothing happens!"

The peasant waves his hat confidently.

Just then a small group of people appears at one end of the village. Catching sight of the mediator, they doff their caps even from a distance; lowering their heads, they slowly approach the district office. A countrywoman walks in front; behind her, a young peasant, and then come the old men.

"What's all this about?" the mediator asks the foreman, looking closely at the people. "Is it that man and his wife again, the ones who want a divorce?"

"The very same, sir," replies the foreman with a smile.

"There you are, my friend," says the mediator to Riazanov, "pay attention: it's the 'woman question'! What do you think of us? We don't lag behind either. Can you imagine, since they were emancipated, a week doesn't go by without some women coming in asking to be divorced from their husbands? What fun!"

The foreman and the clerk laugh.

"Well, so what?" asks Riazanov.

"For me the question gets resolved very simply. Hello, children," he says to the petitioners approaching the porch at that time.

They bow in silence.

"What do you want?"

"We appeal to you, your grace."

A woman sinks to her knees.

"Get up, my dear, get up! No need for that. Tell me your business. Apparently, you went on another binge? So, you men, tell me what this is all about!"

"What's there to say? Semën Semënych, sir! This woman's got completely out of hand."

"You hear what the elders say? What's your name—Malan'ia?"

"Agrafena."

"You hear, Agrafena? Aren't you ashamed?"

The woman doesn't display the least bit of shame; in fact, quite the contrary, she flashes the old men a contemptuous glance. She has one black eye. The mediator is at a bit of loss.

"She don't obey, don't obey at all," one man mumbles from behind.

"She don't look after the livestock, nothing," adds another.

"What a troublemaker she is, this woman, a disaster," confirms the foreman.

The mediator shakes his head.

"All their kin are like that, good for nothing," the foreman remarks.

"How can you be like that, Agrafena? Ah?" the mediator asks.

The woman makes no reply.

"And you, young man, how are you looking after her?" he says, turning to her husband. "You're her husband, you're in charge."

The husband rumples his hair. His face is stupid and sad, his lips thick.

"You should teach your wife to respect her elders," the mediator instructs him. "Yes."

The husband frowns and stares at the ground, holding his cap in his two hands.

"And if your wife won't respect her elders," continues the mediator, "then what'll happen? Is that a good thing? Think about it!"

"I keep telling them," adds the foreman, indicating the petitioners, "that's why it says in our laws: 'You feed your woman and teach your woman!'"

"You're lying," the mediator says, interrupting him. "That's not what it says in our laws; but we have to live together with love and in harmony, because that pleases God."

"That's fair, sir," the foreman affirms.

"Well, yes; but I've no time to yammer with you. You, my dear, must get that nonsense out of your head! If someone starts leading you astray, come and tell him—the foreman. And you, young man, look after your wife and instill in her respect for her elders. Well, now come here, Agrafena, and you, what's your name?"

"Mitry."

"Agrafena and Dmitry, kiss and live according to God's will: love one another, respect your parents, and obey your superiors. God grant you happiness!"

"Semën Semënych!" says the foreman.

"What is it?"

"Have the elders teach her a lesson right now. You should give her a little scare right here in the office."

"No, that's not needed now. And so, friends, go with God!"

The petitioners bow and leave. The foreman and the clerk see the mediator to his carriage.

"Well, that's everything, isn't it?" asks the foreman.

"Everything."

"Are you seated comfortably?"

"Yes."

"Well, God bless! Onward, driver!"

"To hell with you!"

Off they went.

"You can't demand any more from them now," says the mediator to Riazanov.

"I don't demand anything. Besides, one can see some significant success even now."

The conversation didn't go well. Little by little the mediator began humming a romance.

"'Tell her what she's worth to me. . . .' Hello!" he shouts to peasants he meets between lines of the song.

"'It's so hard for me. . . .' Where did you get that?" he sticks his head out of the carriage to ask a peasant carrying a log. The peasant hastily stops his horse, doffs his hat, and shouts: "From Kliuchi."

"What did you pay?"

But he couldn't hear the peasant's answer; he could merely see him tugging at his horse, opening his mouth, and waving his hand.

"'Tell her how terrrribly my heart is aching,'" the mediator croons again.

They ride through the field; the *zemstvo* horses with their mangy tails run nimbly; their legs are shaggy, their ears long.

"Hey, you, hussars," the driver cries cheerfully, flicking them across their frisky legs.

It was getting hot. It was quiet in the field; clusters of white clouds stood still in the sky with hawks hanging in the air above.

The mediator stops his singing—he's overcome with drowsiness; Riazanov's eyes also begin to close. . . .

"Why no greeting? Huh?"

Riazanov opens his eyes: it's a village. A peasant stands near the carriage and the mediator is asking him: "Have your arms fallen off—can't remove your cap? Huh?"

The peasant is silent.

"I don't need your bow," the mediator says to him. "You're being taught some politeness, you fools, for your own good, understand?"

"We understand," replies the peasant, gazing off into the field.

"So that you remember to be polite to everyone from now on, I'm ordering you to spend a day locked up in the barn. My friends," the mediator says, addressing a group of peasants in the distance, "take this boor off to the village elder and tell him that the mediator's ordered him to be locked away in the cooler for a day."

Two peasants come forward, take the boor by the arm, and lead him away, without turning around, escorting him quietly, holding their caps under their arms. The boor spreads his elbows wide and waddles from side to side; his legs are short and his feet are bare.

"Go on," says the mediator to the driver.

"Gee up, my pets," cries the driver dreamily.

They ride on in silence.

"You still can't knock the rudeness out of them," the mediator turns to address Riazanov with a laugh.

"Yes," Riazanov replies.

They came down below a mountain. Another village appears across the river. They encounter peasants from the field, either on horseback or on foot with scythes over their shoulders.

"Hello, lads! Dinnertime, is it?" the mediator asks them.

"Yes, kind sir."

"Enjoy your meal," the mediator cries after them.

They drive into the village. In the very middle of the street lies something large, covered by a piece of canvas.

"Stop! What's this? Driver, open it!"

A peasant's body is lying there and he's wearing a pair of worn-out bast sandals; his belly is swollen, his eyes bulging; there's a cup at his head with a few copper coins in it.

"Hey, woman, whose body's this?"

"A passerby, my dear sir, a passerby. He died some five days ago," the woman replies, approaching the carriage. "God only knows what happened to him. He arrived with a comrade, started taking off his shoes, and then began drinking and drinking. . . ."

"Where's his comrade?"

"Sitting in the hut, wailing."

"Has the lieutenant reported it to the police?"

"Yes, he has."

"And what did he do?"

"God knows."

"Does the deceased smell?"

"Ugh, nasty! He's so swelled up."

"Well, God rest his soul," says the mediator with a sigh, and tosses a small coin into the cup. "Drive on!"

Once more the road leads through a field; it's hot and the horses are raising dust; stunted bushes grow alongside the ravine; in the distance peasants in a row stand in the grass and wave their scythes all together; there's a sparse aspen grove with tussocks, mosquitos, and small puddles of greenish water among the tussocks. The village stands just past the aspens, as if flung onto the slope; beyond the little river stands an old landowner's house with gray walls, green shutters, and a dilapidated wooden fence; a little further, in a hollow, stands another small house, built recently, with a young well-tended garden and a bathhouse on the pond. Further still is the manor house—a long, awkward structure with galleries, columns, broken windows, and a collapsing roof; on the slope one can see another house with a thatched roof, but still a manor house: lean borzois run in the courtyard, turkeys are gobbling, and here and there stand servants with long, oiled sideburns wearing knee-length coats.

"Landowners, yes, landowners live here," says the mediator, as if scrutinizing something.

"Many of them?"

"Like dogs."

"Are they good landowners?" asks Riazanov, after a brief pause.

"Not a chance. To hell with them, these landowners! They're all poor. Ruined! None of them have a pot to pee in."

"In other words, all's lost except their honor."

"No; everything's lost, including their honor. What kind of honor can they have with nothing left? Believe me," the mediator says suddenly, turning to Riazanov, "it's a pity! A pity for their fellow nobles."

"No doubt."

"No, what haven't they done so far, as a matter of fact, what haven't they done to those unfortunate peasants? You can't imagine what sort of people they are. Where they can possibly squeeze the peasants, they do so, never missing a chance."

"Well, and do the peasants miss any chances?"

"Of course, to tell the truth, the peasants stand up for themselves: one way or another, they wear down the landowner."

"In other words, it's mutual exhaustion. Well, and what are you doing here?"

"What? Why, the role of the peace mediator consists in. . . ."

"In what, sir?"

"Well, the investigation of various misunderstandings."

"From what do these misunderstandings arise?"

"You've just seen for yourself: from various infractions and so forth."

"In a word, from property. Isn't that right?"

"Yes, it is."

"That is, one person wishes to acquire something that another person doesn't wish to give away. Is that it?"

"Well, yes."

"So where does the misunderstanding reside? In my heart and soul I would like to give you that thing, but it seems to me that I really don't? Is that it?"

"What do you mean?"

"For example, I take this pillow and think to myself: 'I won't give it to him. It's better if I use it to sleep on.' And then some perspicacious fellow comes and says to me: 'This is a misunderstanding. Although you think you don't want to give this pillow to Semën Semënych, it only seems that way; in your soul you really want to and afterward you'll even be grateful to me that I ordered you to give it to him. Is that so?"

"Of course . . . do you see . . . let me relate one episode to you.

I have an estate here in the district where I'm supposed to carry out land apportionment; so I want to begin, but it turns out this land's belonged to the peasants from time immemorial. Their forefathers purchased it for money earned by the sweat of their brow; but since they themselves belonged to the landowner, and didn't have the legal right to own land, they bought it in the landowner's name. That landowner died a long time ago, and the current owner doesn't want to hear anything about it."

"Well, so then what?"

"So they're going to take it away from the peasants; that is, they won't actually take it, but they'll compel them to redeem it."

"Again?"

"Yes, again. What are you going to do now?"

"And what are you going to do?"

"There's nothing I can do here."

"And the town officials?"

"They can't do anything either because in such cases only written documents can be taken into consideration. No, just imagine my position! I say to the peasants: 'The owner wants to give you this piece of land,' but they reply, 'But all this land is ours.'"

"Are you certain it really belongs to them?"

"Of course. Absolutely certain."

"Yet still you say the owner's giving them that piece of land?"

"Yes, that's what I say. What else can I do?"

"Yes. That's a genuine misunderstanding. Are they all like this?"

"Are what?"

"All the misunderstandings?"

"Almost all of them."

"Hmm. Estimable work."

At that time the carriage came up to the landowner's manor house: it was a new structure with a thatched roof, encircled by a dozen or so young lindens. A new cottage stood not far off, as well as a shed and a barn. The owner was standing outside in the courtyard, gray-haired, wearing a caftan with no hat; he greeted them.

"My compliments to you!" the mediator shouts to him and waves his hand. "He's a detestable fellow," he adds, turning to Riazanov. "That is, he's such a horrible beast, I tell you, you won't be able to find anyone like him in Petersburg for love or money. An outrageous beast! Here's an example of the sort of thing he does: he rented half a *desyatina* of land[4] from someone alongside the road, sowed it with oats, and posted a watchman there to guard it. As soon as the livestock passed by, one or another of them wandered in and nibbled—the watchman grabbed him immediately. Damage! Well, that's a fine. What a rogue he is! You start talking to him, 'If you please,' he says, 'I'm not a wealthy man; everyone can insult me. That's all I have to live on.' So, what can you do with that sort of man? All you can do is spit."

The peasants' backyards were visible behind the manor house along with barns and hemp fields, the blacksmith's shop, and a mill up on the knoll.

"And soon you'll see the home of another peculiar personage," explains the mediator. "Just imagine what he did: when the emancipation was proclaimed, naturally he received the manifesto and read it, and then immediately locked it away in his desk. He says to his peasants: 'If one of you dares to make a peep about this freedom—I'll flog you to death.'"

Just then a landowner's house appears, standing with its back to the forest, painted in an outrageous color with white designs. Dogs spring out of the courtyard and come rushing up to the horses.

"You know what? Let's go have dinner with this gentleman. I have to see him anyway to reach an agreement with his peasants."

Riazanov agrees; the mediator orders the driver to turn in to the courtyard. A woman carrying a washtub of dirty water comes onto the porch.

"Is the master at home?" the mediator asks her.

"He is," she replies, emptying the tub.

"Well, this goose would also be good," the mediator whispers to Riazanov as he climbs out of the carriage. "Our friend, a military man."

---

4.   A measure of land equivalent to 2.7 acres.

There was no one in the entrance, only a hunter's horn and the skin of a wolf hanging on the wall. In the hall, in the middle of the room, stands the master himself, still a young man; his cheek is bandaged and he's complaining of a toothache.

"I can't talk," he says, holding onto his cheek. "Please, sit down."

The mediator asks him about the business matter and hints about dinner.

"It's the third day and I still can't eat a thing—my tooth hurts terr-rribly. But I'll order dinner at once."

They were served vodka and pickles.

"You ought to have it pulled out," advises the mediator.

"Mmm," moans the landowner and waves his arm. "I'm afraid."

The mediator sighs and drinks his vodka down; Riazanov also drinks his. They sit in silence. The landowner paces around the room and spits into the corner. An hour later they bring in cutlets and soft-boiled eggs. They eat.

"Could you possibly summon the peasants?" asks the mediator.

They call them; the mediator goes out onto the porch to see them and to try to reconcile them with the landowner. There aren't many of them, only five in all, but they can't reach an agreement. The mediator returns to the room several times, flushed and perspiring; he hurriedly downs a shot of vodka, and, snacking on some black bread, says to the landowner in a low voice: "You can't do a thing with them. The real problem, damn it, is the blacksmith. Order him to leave!"

"Oh, don't listen to them; you do what's necessary," the landowner replies, first ducking into the corner.

The mediator thinks for a bit, shrugs his shoulders, and heads back out to the porch; but he returns after a few minutes, saying that the peasants are still demanding the meadows. The landowner hears him out without saying a word, then goes out onto the porch, makes some sign with his fingers, and in silence shows it to the peasants. The peasants look and also make no reply.

"Well, so, my fellow Orthodox, you've seen the meadows?" the mediator asks them after the landowner's gone back inside.

"We have," reply the peasants.

"That's the point."

The landowner paces the hall, holding onto his cheek and shaking his head from side to side. Suddenly he turns and goes back to face the peasants; removing the bandage around his jaw, he says right to the blacksmith's face: "If it weren't for my toothache, I'd show you what for. You ought to thank God that my tooth hurts."

The blacksmith retreats.

The negotiations continue until sunset but they are still unable to reach an agreement. At last the mediator gives up and asks for his horses.

They leave. It begins to grow dark.

"Where shall we spend the night?" the mediator asks the driver.

"At the district office, with Pëtr Nikitich. There's nowhere else to go."

"All right."

"It's quiet there," says the driver.

"What?"

"Quiet, I said."

"The hell with that," the mediator says in a disgruntled voice. He was distraught; but, after arriving at the district office, he calmed down a bit.

The clerk, a retired soldier, was just preparing to go to bed. They light a candle and send for the village elder.

"Look," says the mediator to Riazanov. "Pëtr Nikitich will come soon. He's a smart one, he's—like a government minister! Well, are there any unresolved issues?" he asks the clerk, who is already standing at attention near the door.

"None at all, yar'exlency."

"In other words, all's well?"

"Precisely so, yar'exlency."

"So you see," says the mediator to Riazanov, smiling with self-satisfaction. "I know full well that everything's in order with Pëtr Nikitich: not one complaint, no squabbles, no drunkenness, nothing."

"So then, is there a temperance society here, or what?" asks Riazanov.

"No, what sort of society? In the third district the peasants were about to take the pledge (this was before me, by the way); well, and what happened? They exchanged blows just on account of that and then nothing came of it. Now such drunkenness has resulted, it's like nothing you've ever seen! But there's no drunkenness here, thanks to Pëtr Nikitich's good management."

During all this time the clerk was standing motionless at the door and approached the desk only occasionally; he would spit on his fingers carefully, trim the wick promptly, and then return to the door; if he had to cough or blow his nose, he would go into the entranceway. It was stuffy in the room; the pendulum ticked slowly, scraping and brushing against something; flies rested on the walls; on the street, somewhere far away, singing could be heard; someone was puttering about, breathing heavily in the entranceway. . . .

"Well, shall we turn in?" says the mediator with a yawn, but just then, with even footsteps, the village elder came in, bowed, and stood in the middle of the room.

"There, sir! I recommend him," says the mediator, pointing to him.

The village elder, a short, solid peasant with graying hair and a placid face, bows once again, and clasping his arms behind his back, remains silent.

"Well, Pëtr Nikitich, how are things? Is all well?" asks the mediator.

"All's well, sir," replies the elder calmly.

"Why even ask? Is there ever a time when all's not well with you?"

"It happens, sir."

"Well, enough of that!"

The elder smiles respectfully.

"And as for that document that I sent, well? Is it signed?"

"Yes, sir."

"In other words, with no hesitation?"

"None at all, sir."

"Excellent! No, let me tell you a story about him," says the mediator to Riazanov. "There was a holiday here in the village; the peasants, as usual, drank too much. And, I must say, he'd warned them before-hand: 'Watch out,' he says, 'there's a holiday coming. You can drink, enjoy yourselves as you like; just so there won't be any outrageous scenes.' Fine. Well, the peasants got so drunk that many of them wound up lying in the street. He had them all gathered up and put into the barn. The next day, naturally, they were all suffering from hangovers. My Pëtr Nikitich conducts them to the church, leads them to the portico on their knees, and orders them all to make one hundred prostrations: 'Pray!' he says. 'I won't punish you, but pray to God that He forgives for yesterday's outrageous behavior! Well, there was nothing they could do; they bow as they were told, and he stands there counting. Well, I can tell you, the peasants said to me, 'It would've been better if he'd given us twenty-five lashes with a birch rod, instead of making us do all that bowing, because, don't you see, what that does to a head with a hangover?' Yes, he's an excellent fellow, that Pëtr Nikitich is," says the mediator, slapping him across the shoulders.

Pëtr Nikitich smiles serenely.

"Well, my friend, how shall we set up our beds?"

"I had them prepared out in the courtyard. It'll be quieter."

"Splendid, my friend."

"Do you have any orders?"

"No, my friend; what sort of orders? We'll talk tomorrow."

The village elder wishes him a good night and leaves.

"My friend, you should go to bed, too," the mediator says to the clerk.

"Yes, yar'exlency," replies the clerk and makes a left turn and goes to bed. The mediator leaves. Riazanov sits there for a while, and then also goes out to the courtyard. Someone was wandering around and fumbling about in the dark.

"Who's there?" asks Riazanov.

"It's me," says the mediator and sings: "Tra-ra-ta-ta."

Riazanov walks across the courtyard. A bed had been made up there under an awning. He is about to get undressed but goes back to the room to fetch his coat. In the entranceway he bumps into the driver, whom the mediator tries to send packing: "You, my dear fellow, go sleep with the horses!"

"I'll just grab my homespun coat. Agaf'ia, wait a bit, where is it, my coat?" the driver was saying in a sleepy voice, searching for it in the dark. "Ah, damn it! Here it is! Why'd you take my coat away? Agaf'ia!"

Early the next morning Riazanov was sitting in the room drinking tea while the mediator was chatting with the peasants in the entranceway; he enters the room, takes a gulp of tea from his glass, and leaves again, still irritated about something. The peasants object at first, but then get quieter and quieter; they finally calm down completely; only one gloomy, monotonous voice continues to answer the mediator in an impassive and steady way. This voice doesn't cease. The mediator begins to get angry and shout even more—the voice keeps on. . . . All of a sudden. . . .

"Hey, you!"

Whop, whop, whop—the sound rings out in the entranceway and the voice falls silent. It becomes very quiet.

Riazanov, without finishing his glass of tea, picks up his cap and leaves the room. In the entranceway stands a crowd of peasants and the enraged mediator; the peasant is getting up off the floor, rolling his eyes wildly. . . . Some distance away stands Pëtr Nikitich, hands behind his back, just as serene and self-assured.

Riazanov goes out into the street, turns into the first gate, and hires a peasant to drive him back to the Shchetinins'.

He arrived there that evening. Mar'ia Shchetinina caught a glimpse of him from the window, turned pale, and ran out onto the porch. "What happened?" she cried, extending her arms.

"Nothing much," replied Riazanov calmly. "He got into a fight there. . . . So, I just up and left. Good luck to him!"

Shchetinin also came out onto the porch. "What's the matter?"

"It's that he's . . . he's come back," Mar'ia Nikolavna said, gasping for breath. She was unable to conceal her delight.

Shchetinin regarded her coolly, then looked at Riazanov, and returned to his room.

CHAPTER XI

———

MAR'IA NIKOLAVNA WAS SITTING IN THE HALL PLAYING chords on the piano with one hand; Riazanov was pacing the room; the setting sun was shining directly into the window.

"So, didn't Aleksandr Vasil'ich say anything to you?" asked Mar'ia Nikolavna, bending over the piano.

"Nothing. Why?"

"No. I merely asked."

She played a few more chords and then stopped. "You know," she said, "you did a good thing by leaving."[1]

"What's good about it?"

"You see, the entire district will find out. It'll cause a scandal. That's what's good."

"I didn't think about that at all."

Riazanov began pacing again. Mar'ia Nikolavna, musing and smiling at the same time, said to herself: "I like that very, very much." Then she placed her finger to her lips, thought a little while, and

———

1. *Author's note:* The mediator.

said just as quietly, "Very much. . . . In general, it's all good." Then she suddenly struck the piano keys and began playing *La Marseillaise*[2] loudly and with passionate intensity. These sounds transformed her in a moment: her eyes sparkled, she sat up straight, and she raised her head. Knitting her brows ominously, she confidently moved her lovely tanned hands. After making the sudden last transition, she pressed the pedal and struck the keys with new force. Her entire face shone with unprecedented courage. . . . She cast a self-assured, challenging glance at Riazanov and ceased playing.

Riazanov also stopped pacing. "Here's what habit does," he said, approaching the piano. "You just played a march and immediately it seemed to me that right here, next to me, stood a sergeant-major repeating: 'Left, right, left, right. . . .'"

"What makes you recollect those sergeant-majors?" Mar'ia Nikolavna replied with displeasure.

"Well, from time to time, nothing. It arouses my memories."

Mar'ia Nikolavna looked at him and asked: "Do you know what march that is?"

"I do."

"So what are you saying?"

"I'm not saying anything."

"However, you must agree," she said standing up, "that marches vary."

"Indeed, they do."

"And this one, for example, is nothing like the Darmstadt march."[3]

"Naturally. But, whatever it is, it's still a march; consequently, sooner or later, you'll hear: 'Halt! Dress right! Attention!' You can never forget that."

"I won't forget it."

"Exactly. There's no reason to get upset."

2. The national anthem of France, written and composed in 1792 during the French Revolutionary Wars and adopted in 1795.

3. Presumably an imperial as opposed to revolutionary march.

Mar'ia Nikolavna fell silent; after standing in front of Ria-zanov for a while and thinking about something, she went over to the window and looked at the sun, which at that moment was merely a red ball sinking behind the forest with its the lower edge already touching the jagged treetops; she stood there for a few moments without batting an eye, staring at the sun, which lit up her face with its ominous reddish light.

"Do you understand what I'm doing?" she asked without stirring.

"What?"

"I want to stare *it* down." She pointed at the sun. "You know there's an old game—to see who can stare down whom."

Riazanov made no reply; leaning his shoulder against the door-post, he looked at her sideways: she stood still as before, resting both her hands on the back of a chair, leaning her head back slightly, bathed by warm light. She continued staring stubbornly at the sun, almost with impudence. At last the expression on her face became more strained and she knitted her brows; all of a sudden she blinked rapidly, covered her eyes with her hands, and turned away from the window.

"Well, who won?" asked Riazanov.

"I couldn't stare it down," she replied with a laugh.

Riazanov also moved away from the window.

"What a foolish thing just occurred to me," she continued, without opening her eyes. "As I was staring at the sun, I recalled how I used to be frightened by the Lord God when I was a little child: they told me I couldn't look at Him either."

"Did you believe it?"

"No, I didn't believe it then either. I found it all so amusing. My nanny had a little icon: God the Father sitting up in the air; but the air was shown as so ugly, it looked as if the Lord of Hosts[4] was sitting on eggs. My nanny would sometimes try to frighten me with Him, but I wasn't afraid of anything. Whenever I looked at Him, I'd start laughing."

---

4.   One of the names of God when regarded as having the angelic forces at his command.

"Aren't you afraid of Him now?"

"Of course not."

"Is that so? Think long and hard! Maybe you're just pretending to be so brave."

"What nonsense! Not only don't I fear Him, I'm not afraid of you either. I merely . . . respect you. . . ."

She uttered these last words almost in a whisper, as if unintentionally defending what she said; at the same time she cast a swift, anxious glance at Riazanov.

He stood with his eyes cast down, tugging at his beard.

"Let's go somewhere," she said suddenly, starting toward the door.

"Where?"

"Somewhere or other, it doesn't matter; but let's go away from here!"

Riazanov stared at her fixedly.

"Why can't you stand being here? What's hampering you?"

"Everything: the walls, the ceiling, everything. I want to leave now, somewhere far, far away. . . ." She paused. "You know that I can't see you at all now," she said squinting. "Instead of a face, you have a green spot. Oh, how very strange! Well, let's go!"

She ran from the terrace into the garden and turned around: Riazanov was walking down the stairs slowly and pensively, still tugging at his beard with one hand. She waited for him; when he caught up with her, she asked: "What do you think, does Aleksandr Vasil'ich fear God or not?"

"I think he does."

Just at that moment Shchetinin entered the hall with soft steps and a gloomy face; thrusting his hands into his pockets, he stopped in the doorway. Then he went out onto the terrace and began walking down the stairs, but he stopped on the last step and looked after Mar'ia Nikolavna and Riazanov; he rubbed his finger on his nose, thought for a bit, and went back inside.

CHAPTER XII

———

THE HEAT WAS STILL INTENSE; THE HARVEST WAS UNDER way. Conversations continued between Mar'ia Nikolavna and Riazanov: there was no end to them.

"Good Lord, what on earth will come of it," Shchetinin wonders aloud to himself, while pacing from corner to corner in his study.

It's noon. Riazanov is sitting on the grass in the shade on the lakeshore and, without stirring, is staring at the water; the sun is baking; on the other bank, from under the bushes, one can see white sand overgrown with burdock; a heron stands at the water's edge, glancing around timidly; somewhere someone is playing a peasant pipe. A few feet from Riazanov, leaning her shoulder against a tree, stands Mar'ia Nikolavna holding a parasol; lustrous shadows glide slowly, almost unnoticeably, across her face and her white dress. Her eyes are half-open—it is hard for her to look directly into the light; she is exhausted by the heat and the heavy noonday quiet. They are both silent.

"When will this summer end?" she asks, gazing forlornly into the distance. "If only I could go away somewhere."

"It doesn't matter: summer's hot everywhere," Riazanov replies after a brief silence.

They are silent again.

"I can imagine what these unfortunate countrywomen experience as they harvest in this heat."

"Yes, indeed."

"Awful!"

"You should buy them parasols."

Mary Nikolavna frowns, then suddenly lowers her parasol, and fastens it. "I don't want to use a parasol anymore. I'll give it to Polia."

Riazanov smiles. "Whom does that spite?"

"No one, only myself."

"It won't make it any easier for them."

"Who?"

"The countrywomen. They still won't have parasols."

Mar'ia Nikolavna is silent; clenching her teeth firmly, she pokes the parasol fitfully into the ground.

"Why are you damaging someone else's parasol?"

"Whose?"

"You said it now belongs to Polia."

"That's . . . I don't know what this is all about," Mar'ia Nikolavna says, lifting her head swiftly, then heads for home.

It's twilight. Riazanov is sitting in his room by the window, leaning on his elbows, looking into the garden. Mar'ia Nikolavna approaches his window from the garden.

"Why are you sitting here?"

Riazanov lifts his elbows.

"I'm so bored!" she says.

"You ought to take up music."

"What nonsense! You think music would help?"

"Or read a book!"

"Your suggestions aren't any good."

"What do you want?"

"I myself don't know," she says. "It's all so . . . I feel very sad."

Riazanov makes no reply.

"You understand," she says speaking rapidly, "I know that none of this will lead anywhere, that one must do something, quickly, very quickly. . . . Well, perhaps it won't succeed . . . suffering. . . . So what? It doesn't matter. . . . At least you know what it's for. Otherwise, what's it all about? I want to live. Why don't you say something?"

"What would you have me say?"

"Say something!"

"What can I possibly say of significance in reply to this: judge for yourself!"

"Well, at least say something insignificant!"

"What's the sense in that?"

"It's all sense, sense. . . ."

"You're a strange woman! But you yourself are striving to make sense."

"Well, yes, yes. Of course. Don't listen to me. I don't know what I'm talking about. Goodbye!"

It's evening. Mar'ia Nikolavna is sitting on the terrace preparing tea; Riazanov is at the other end scanning the newspapers that had just been delivered. Shchetinin enters, casts an offhand glance at them, stands for a few minutes in the middle of the terrace, yawns, and then says: "The evenings have become cooler. It's too damp, I think, for a stroll."

Silence.

"Don't pour me any tea: I don't want it," he says to his wife.

She quietly sets his glass aside. "And what about you? Would you like some?" she asks Riazanov.

"What's that?" he asks, coming to his senses.

"Would you like some tea?"

"Yes, I would." He approaches the table; peering at Shchetinin, he pulls up a chair for himself.

Shchetinin musingly drums his fingers on the table.

"Well, what's in the papers?" he asks, not looking at Riazanov.

"Nothing special; all's well in internal affairs: the pacification program is proceeding successfully, the peasants are being emancipated, banks are being established, and *zemstvo* assemblies are meeting. Well, and in European politics, some small embarrassment has arisen because Napoleon had a friendly tête-à-tête with Bismarck."[1]

Mar'ia Nikolavna smiles; Shchetinin sits, resting his cheek on his hand, looking at the small cakes; then he picks up one of them, breaks it, and asks: "Why has our Stepan started making such poor cakes—they're like nothing on earth; it's as if they're made of wood."

No one makes any reply to this.

"Masha, you ought to say something to him."

"Tell him yourself."

Shchetinin, without turning his head, merely raising his eyebrows and looking askance, stares at his wife for a long time; she is very carefully drinking her tea.

"Awwwmm," Shchetinin forces a yawn. "When are we going to make time to go into the forest?" he starts up again after waiting a little while. "We were planning and planning, but we never got around to it. Ivan Pavlych and his wife also wanted to go with us."

"What forest?" Mar'ia Nikolavna remarks in a low voice.

"No; it would be nice, you know, to take a drive out, have tea, relax. Huh? What do you think, Riazanov?"

"Yes, not bad."

"There, you see! He agrees, too, Masha!"

"What?"

"He'll go with us, too!"

"Well, let him go. What do I care?"

"But you yourself used to like that before."

---

1. Louis-Napoléon Bonaparte (1808–1873) was the first president of the French Republic and, as Napoleon III, the ruler of the Second French Empire. He was the nephew and heir of Napoleon I. Beginning in 1866 he had to face the mounting power of Prussia, as Chancellor Otto von Bismarck sought German unification under Prussian leadership.

"That was before!"

"No; I thought . . . in a word . . . the devil only knows how awful it is here . . . stuffy," says Shchetinin, suddenly yanking off his necktie and standing up from the table. "Autumn will come," he says, talking to himself, now standing at the other end of the terrace, gazing out into the garden, "and we still have to plant some acacias, or else it looks kind of . . . empty. Here come those damned peasants again," he utters irritably, having noticed some peasants approaching the porch. "Why won't they ever leave me in peace?" he says, grabbing hold of his head and walking away.

Silence ensues on the terrace once more. Riazanov, after reading a letter, examines the envelope.

"What are you scrutinizing?" Mar'ia Nikolavna asks him.

"I'm looking at the seal. These days they've started to use such bad sealing wax."[2]

"What do you mean?"

"It doesn't hold."

"Listen: how much does it cost to get from here to St. Petersburg?"

"That depends on how you go."

"Well, the least expensive way?"

"About fifty rubles."

"That's all? It's not much."

"Don't tell me you're planning to go?"

"I don't know. Why?"

"Nothing. . . ."

Mar'ia Nikolavna stares at him intently. "What would you say if I were to go, too?"

"I wouldn't say anything. I don't know why you'd go."

"You don't?"

"No."

"Hmm."

Mar'ia Nikolavna's face assumes a carefree expression; she stands up from the table and, humming some song, approaches the

---

2. A veiled reference to the fact that the censors were opening his mail.

terrace railing; she stands there a long time, leaning on it with both hands, squinting as she surveys the picture stretched out broadly below the garden: she looks at the blue lakes enveloped in evening mist, the lilac clusters of clouds gathered in the west, and the pale sky gradually growing cooler. . . . A quiet, dewy night has already descended on the garden and it's absolutely still in the courtyard; the only sound is that of Ivan Stepanych playing his violin in the annex, "How glorious is Our Lord in Zion."[3]

"Have you ever been in love?" Mar'ia Nikolavna asks, suddenly turning to Riazanov.

"No."

She looks him in the eye for a long time with distrust. "Why not?"

"There was no one to love."

She slowly turns her back to him; leaning her face over the railing, she asks in almost a whisper: "And now?"

"N-n. . . ."

"Are we going to have supper or what?" Shchetinin asks, unexpectedly coming in the door.

It's Sunday. In the morning, the priest arrives after mass and brings Mar'ia Nikolavna some communion bread. Breakfast is served.

"Why do you visit our church so rarely?" he asks her.

"Would you like some vodka?" she asks the priest.

He makes no reply to this question, merely wheezes; hitching up his right sleeve, he reaches for the decanter.

"It's hot, father," says Shchetinin.

"Very warm, sir," he replies, spreading some butter on a piece of bread.

Shchetinin paces the room; Mar'ia Nikolavna sits at the table and absentmindedly crumbles some bread.

---

3. The official hymn of the Russian Empire. The words were written by the classical author M. M. Kheraskov (1733–1807) and set to music by the composer D. S. Bortyansky (1751–1825).

After drinking his shot of vodka, the priest bites off a piece of bread; looking at the marks left on the butter by his teeth, he asks:

"That fellow, what's his name? Mr. . . . the student . . . is he still here?"

"Yes," Shchetinin replies faintly and immediately asks the priest, "How are your affairs?"

"My affairs, sir? Not so good."

"What's the matter?"

"I can't cope with my cow in any way: she doesn't give any milk, so I have to think she's lacking it entirely. And my wife's not quite right—she's always complaining about her stomach."

"That's not good," Shchetinin remarks, and again starts pacing the room from corner to corner.

"I'm exhausted," says the priest, sitting himself down at the table. "Oh, my God! It's a hot day, and besides that, I had to deliver a sermon."

"What sermon?" Shchetinin asks with sympathy, obviously thinking about something else.

"I made a few remarks. To tell the truth, I've had that sermon on hand for a while; I inherited it from my late father-in-law. Well, still, be that as it may. Impossible. Strong measures were taken. . . ."

"What was that sermon about?" asks Mar'ia Nikolavna.

"The love of wisdom."

"What?"

"The love of wisdom, madam," the priest repeats briskly.

"What's that? Does it mean someone who likes to be clever?" she asks with a smile.[4]

"Well, yes, ma'am, clever," replies the priest, also smiling. "You yourself know what sort of times we live in. Just a few days ago the archpriest at the cathedral in town was telling me—the Right-Reverend had summoned him—well, he, he says, he, he says, he went on and on, he did, and on some more; if, he says, if I hear anything

---

4. The Russian calque *liubomudrie* is a compound word usually translated as "philosophy"; like the English word, it means literally "love of wisdom."

about this, I'll grind you to a powder, you'll rot away as a sexton, he says; so I, says the archpriest—what do you think?—I barely got away; I couldn't find the door, he says. I couldn't, and that's that. Luckily, a lay brother showed me out. That's how things are. That's where pride leads us," the priest concludes, addressing Shchetinin.

"Yes," remarks Shchetinin.

"Would you like a little more?" Mar'ia Nikolavna asks him, pointing to the decanter.

The priest looks at it with an inquisitive glance. "Hmm. How can I put it? It's true that. . . . Just a little to drown my sorrows? Ha, ha, ha!"

The priest drinks another shot. "Yes; they're strict, very strict today with these practices," he said, sniffing the bread crust. "Oof! They're strict."

"We can't do without strictness," Shchetinin says casually as he walks past the table.

The priest turns around. "It's fine for you to say, Aleksandr Vasil'ich, that we can't do without it. But let me tell you about our affairs nowadays."

Shchetinin pauses. "You mean about the archpriest?"

"Yes. What do you think about him?"

"So what is it?"

"It's just that in olden times, for example, I come in to present some books, or those birth certificates—I'd bring him a goose, well, if there were many things, I'd bring him a piglet or fifty ko-pecks in cash. And he used to be very pleased! But now, I just try and mention a piglet—he covers me with shame. 'What do you think,' he says, 'you've come to see some clerk or what?' A bottle of rum, a pound of tea, and in addition, three silver rubles. You look, and these birth certificates now cost you six silver rubles if they cost a kopeck. It's true. That's what. New practices. And if a cleric wants to have a little drink," the priest suddenly begins again, now changing his tone, "it'll be in the same proportion. What of it?"

"Be my guest," says Mar'ia Nikolavna.

The priest pours himself a shot, and holding it up to the light, he asks: "Is it gentry vodka?"

"It is," replies Shchetinin.

"Penetrating, devil take it," observes the priest, shaking his head; then he drinks it down and pushes the decanter away decisively. "The heck with it!"

Shchetinin continues to pace the room, apparently deeply concerned about something, almost paying no attention to what is happening around him. From time to time he would pause, glance absentmindedly out the window, ruffle the hair on the back of his head, utter "Yes" to himself, and then resume pacing. Mar'ia Nikolavna follows him impassively with her eyes and in general looks bored; the priest is silent, begins to sigh, and suddenly decides to leave. Just then Riazanov comes in. Mar'ia Nikolavna grows livelier and proposes that they walk the priest home. Riazanov agrees. Mar'ia Nikolavna picks up her parasol, but then tosses it aside and hurriedly fastens a kerchief on her head. They leave.

As they are descending the stairs, the priest casts a sidelong glance at Riazanov, then at Mar'ia Nikolavna, and says with a sigh, "What a sin!"

They'd hardly had time to move away from the porch when Mar'ia Nikolavna, catching up to Riazanov, begins asking him: "Where in the world were you all day yesterday? How is it that I didn't see you?"

"Mar'ia Nikolavna!" cries the priest from behind.

She looks back. The priest closes one eye, raises a finger, and says: "Don't trust him—he'll deceive you."

She smiles and once again begins talking with Riazanov.

"Yesterday I looked all over the garden for you."

They go out to the street.

"Bad conduct," says the priest, following behind them. "That's what we'll write: very bad. Pride, vanity, arrogance, conceit, retribution. . . . Very bad."

Mar'ia Nikolavna walks along without paying him any attention.

"Mr. Riazanov!"

He turns around.

"*Quo usque tandem, Catilina. . . .* How long, then. . . . Do you know Latin? Huh? How can you not know it? *Patientia nostra*[5] . . . *utor, abutor, abuti*[6]—to test, tempt. It's bad, my friend, watch out! And you, madam, should. . . . But excuse me!"

"What are you talking about?" asks Riazanov, leaving Mar'ia Nikolavna.

"Shh!"

The priest takes Riazanov by the arm and with a wink of his eye indicates Mar'ia Nikolavna.

"'Thou shalt not covet!'[7] Understand? I see you're a fine fellow, but you're behaving recklessly. You must be more self-effacing! You know the proverb, 'If you're riding someone else's horse, you have to dismount even in midstream.'[8] You've sinned, well, that's that. *Tacete!*[9] Shh. 'Then Samson went to Gaza.'[10] There's nothing more to say."

"You'd be better off going to bed," says Riazanov.

"And I will. I'm a little tipsy. . . . What can you expect from me, a drunken priest? We're not learned men."

"Goodbye, father," says Mar'ia Nikolavna, pausing near the church.

"Goodbye, madam! Excuse me, for heaven's sake. And you,"

---

5. "*Quo usque tandem abutere, Catilina, patientia nostra?*" [How long, O Catiline, will you abuse our patience?] (Lat.) From a speech given by Cicero, the consul of Rome, in 63 BCE, exposing the plot of Catiline and his allies to overthrow the Roman government.

6. To use, to abuse, abused (Lat.).

7. The first words of the tenth commandment from Exodus 20: "Thou shalt not covet thy neighbor's house, thou shalt not covet thy neighbor's wife."

8. An old Russian saying derived from the *Russkaia Pravda* (1018), the legal code of Kievan Rus' and the subsequent principalities during the time of feudal division.

9. Silence! (Lat.)

10. A quotation from Judges 16:1, "Then went Samson to Gaza, and saw there an harlot, and went in unto her."

he turns to Riazanov, "you won't be forgiven. I'll be forgiven everything, but not you. Never ever. It's not possible. It's impossible to forgive you because you have so much arrogance. That's what. Adieu!"

The priest waves goodbye and locks the gate behind him.

After parting with the priest, they walk along side by side and both are silent. The path they followed leads to the mill. Locked as a result of the holiday, the water echoes below, forcing its way through slits in the water gate; ducks are paddling around in the pond. After making it across the dam, they find themselves on the other side of the river, on the sandy bank, in the bushes. The noonday sun scorches the broad water-meadows, strewn with green tussocks and dark pools of water covered over in green slime; the opposite hilly bank of the river can be seen clearly through the transparent rippling air; it is thickly overgrown with low forest and suffused with bright noonday light. Mar'ia Nikolavna pauses amid the bushes and sits down on the grass. Riazanov also sits down.

"It's lovely here," she says, making herself comfortable in the shade.

Riazanov lowers himself onto his elbow and looks around.

Mar'ia Nikolavna thinks a bit and smiles. "It's very odd," she says, "that all this merely amuses me now. Really. Even that priest. It's so much fun!" She turns toward the water that is shining brightly between the bushes and greedily inhales the cool fresh air. "It's nice here," she repeats. "Cool, yet over there, it's so hot on the hill. Look at the trees. You see how they stand and are completely still. They've been made motionless by intense heat. Huh?"

"I see."

"And the grass looks so red," she says, squinting. "It's thin grass . . . and there's a bald spot on the mound. There's a horse in the hazel-grove. You see, it's a skewbald. She's hot, too, poor thing. . . . You know what would be nice now," she pauses and then continues, "it would be nice, you know, to go up along the river, get a little further, and hide in the reeds. It's so quiet there! Huh? Let's go," she says suddenly, standing up decisively.

"What an idea you've come up with! Besides, the boat has cracks in it: it leaks."

"So what?"

"You'll get wet."

"Whatever! Who cares?"

"As you like."

"Here's what we'll do: we'll head out there, beyond the islands, and then let the boat float along in the current; let it take us wherever it wants."

"But we won't get beyond the dams. We'll wind up back here again."

"However," she says after pondering, "however, as a matter of fact, I've been carried away . . . by my imagination. Let's go home! It's time to return. Still, I've enjoyed myself," she begins talking again after they'd crossed the dam. "Today I feel particularly cheerful. I want to make peace with everyone, to forgive all my enemies. Is that possible? What do you think? To conclude a temporary truce for one day? One day only? Huh? Is it possible?"

"Do you know why good military commanders conclude temporary truces?"

"Why?"

"So that under the guise of friendship they can scrutinize the enemy's position and allow their troops to get some rest."

"Well, I, too, wish to scrutinize his position; let's go back through the village," she says laughing. Turning off the road, she walks past the barns toward the soldiers' quarters.

"With whom are you at war, I'm curious to know," asks Riazanov.

"For now, with myself."

"Ah."

The place where they were walking was remote, even though it was located close to a large village: there was a slope, a puddle with mucky banks below, and a little mucky bridge. Some children who are hoisting up their pants are wandering around the puddle; several bowed white willows line the shore; through their sparse leaves one can see tiny white cottages of soldiers' wives, grouped together, clinging somehow to the hillside; there were vegetable gardens where trees stood here and there damaged and soiled by birds; sparrows noisily swarmed from the derelict wattle fencing. Further on, a ravine led off in one direction, overgrown with stunted shrubs; in it lay a dead horse devoured by dogs. In the other direction were the peasants' barns and the village.

Mar'ia Nikolavna stops on the small landing; raising her hand to shield her eyes, she looks around. "I haven't been here in a long time," she says, as if surprised by something.

The farther they walk, the more serious her face becomes, the more carefully and nervously she begins glancing from side to side, as if she'd inadvertently come to some new, unfamiliar place and didn't at all recognize where she was.

The deserted village street, brightly lit by the sun, is lifeless and empty: here and there peasants are wandering around by the gates; peasant women and girls, hiding in the shade, are checking each other's heads for nits; little girls had climbed into the frame of a new cottage and are sitting there, wailing the words of some song as loud as they can; jackdaws perch motionless on the roofs, dazed by the heat.

Mar'ia Nikolavna removes the kerchief from her head and walks in the shade past the courtyards. Riazanov follows her, looking down at the ground.

At one lane, near the wattle fence, sits a group of girls who are just about to strike up a song, "With a hey, and a ho. . . ." But noticing the two of them, the girls stop. Mar'ia Nikolavna goes up to the girls and asks gently: "Why did you stop?"

The girls stand up.

"Why don't you sing?"

The girls make no reply and look away.

"We'd like to hear you," Mar'ia Nikolavna adds, now not so firmly.

The girls suddenly begin giggling, cover their noses, and quiet down behind one another.

Mar'ia Nikolavna regards them with compassion, then looks at Riazanov, and moves on.

The girls burst out laughing. Mar'ia Nikolavna turns around—they hide and all of a sudden the whole group of them sets off running away from her toward the barn. Mar'ia Nikolavna frowns a little and then goes on.

After passing several courtyards, she pauses and begins examining one cottage. It is very old, with only one window, and is propped up on both sides with braces; a blind old nag with a sagging lower lip and a scraggly mane is staring through the open gate. It stands right at the gate, shaking her head from side to side, waggles her ears a bit. In front of the cottage stands a boy about four years old holding a long switch in his hands.

Mar'ia Nikolavna goes up to the boy and strokes his head; the boy doesn't budge from his place and doesn't stir.

"Where's your mother?" Mar'ia Nikolavna asks him.

He makes no reply and doesn't even look at her; he merely shrugs his shoulders and tries to reach his cheek with his tongue; then he tosses his switch aside and goes into the cottage. Mar'ia Nikolavna glances through the gates: the courtyard is filled with all sorts of trash; a hen sits on an overturned wooden plough.

"Mama go-ed to Auntie Matliëna," the same lad yells suddenly from the window.

Mar'ia Nikolavna goes up to the window; but it is so dark in the cottage that it is impossible to see anything inside; it smells of cold cinders and she can hear another child crying somewhere inside. Mar'ia Nikolavna begins looking more closely and gradually is able to discern dark walls, a homespun coat on a bench, an empty pot and a cradle hanging inside the cottage; in the cradle sits an infant covered over with flies. He stops crying and looks at Mar'ia Nikolavna in surprise; the lad she'd first seen at the gate is now rocking the cradle and keeps saying: "Listen! Mama's comin' vewy soon. Hear?"

"Is this your brother?" asks Mar'ia Nikolavna.

"That's Vaska," replies the boy.

The boy sitting in the cradle grabs its edge and shakes his head from side to side, gawking in fear at Mar'ia Nikolavna. He looks and stares, and then suddenly begins coughing, bursts into tears, and starts yelling. . . .

"He's sick," explains the boy and begins rocking him again.

Mar'ia Nikolavna wants to ask something more, but she looks through the window, thinks a bit, and leaves. The blind nag is still standing at the gate, waggling her ears, casually smacking her sagging lip.

Next to this cottage stands another, just the same, and further on, more of them: rotting gray roofs, dark windows with the smell of cinders and the sound of children's squeals; crooked gates and rickety wattle fences are full of holes with hempen shirts hanging on them. There are almost no people around; only Mishka the fool, standing in the middle of the street, his crazy eyes bulging, his mouth dribbling spit, is shaking his head and singing, "La-la-la."

Mar'ia Nikolavna walks faster and faster, drops her eyes and tries as best she can not to look from side to side.

"Why have you become so dejected?" Riazanov asks her in jest.

She makes no reply, merely looks at him with her sad, dark eyes, and then lowers them again to the ground.

"And what about that truce? Or have you reconsidered?"

"I have," she says quietly, shaking her head, walking on even faster.

At the very end of the village, next to the district office, a crowd has gathered. Mar'ia Nikolavna stops an old woman and asks: "What are they doing there?"

"God knows, my dear. Must be some sort of court case. Something between them."

Mar'ia Nikolavna is about to keep walking, but then stops, thinks a bit, and walks around the fire shed; she creeps up to the wattle fence from behind and watches. Riazanov follows and also begins watching. Everything that is happening in the courtyard can be seen through the cracks in the fence: the village elder is sitting on the porch in his shirtsleeves; not far from him, leaning on their sticks, stand old men in their dirty hats sporting horse brasses on their homespun shirts; beyond them stands the crowd. From time to time the clerk appears on the porch; he argues with the peasants and shouts to someone: "No, first go comb your hair! Comb your hair, you hear me? After that I'll talk to you," and he leaves again. The peasants shout something after him and argue among themselves. At first it is impossible to make anything out, but then, little by little, the matter becomes clear: the quarrel is over the assessments; the crowd argues and is growing angry; the authorities don't meddle in this affair; the village elder, sitting on a step, keeps yawning and glancing from side to side distractedly; the old men chat among themselves, poking their sticks at the ground. But right there, next to the wall, only a little distance away from the rest, stand two other peasants without hats who aren't taking part in the argument. One of them, tall, dark-skinned, with a broad, gloomy face, folding his arms across his chest and leaning forward slightly, listens carefully to what the crowd is saying, anxiously twisting his head to position first his right ear, then his left; at the same time he is raising, lowering, and shifting his thick dark eyebrows; the other peasant has a womanish face, limp, with a little thin fair beard and small red eyes. He is looking up calmly, very carefully observing some sparrows: how they hop across the roof of the fire shed and chirp as loud as they can, trying to steal a bread crust away from each other. He even finds this amusing. . . .

"Well, what will it be, lads?" one old man asks loudly, walking away from the wall and looking at the large crowd. "No matter how long we keep talking, still, it's like. . . ."

Both peasants are startled and stand up straight.

"No, wait a minute! No, stop," people in the crowd start yelling.

"Why stand there? We should give 'em a good thrashin' and be done with it."

"Good idea. What else do we need?" confirms another.

"There's no need to encourage 'em."

"Why encourage 'em?"

"Why even look at them? Yes, it's about time."

"Look at them or not, we all have to pay the assessment for them."

"They're clever ones."

"If the commune pays it for 'em they'll be very happy."

"What, ya' think they'll start cryin'? Ah, my lads," someone says in jest.

They all start laughing, and even the village elder inquires: "Wha's going on?"

"We're sayin', sir, maybe ya' should give 'em a little scare. It'd be better," one little peasant declares humbly.

"It wouldn't hurt," confirms the elder and yawns again.

"For fear, so they knew to fear," observes one old man.

"And afterward they'll even say thanks," the little peasant adds.

"As usual."

Suddenly they all fall silent; it becomes very quiet; the only thing you can hear is some old man coughing and someone else muttering to himself in a disgruntled voice: "Hey, you . . . what on earth . . . so that. . . ." The dark-browed peasant is squinting and trying to hide and doesn't budge from his spot; the other one, with his mouth half-open, his head tilted back, also stands there motionless. . . . But then the village elder stands up; stretching first, he utters: "Well then, if we're to give them a beating, let's do it. Why wait around?"

The crowd sways; the two holdouts, standing by the wall, both look at the village elder at the same time and drop their eyes. An incoherent conversation starts up again; someone shouts, "Wait a bit," but no one hears anything else; the crowd surges, the peasants climb up on the porch, lose their way, and a few of them go out of the gate. A militiaman comes out of the district office carrying two bunches of switches under his arm; they clear him some space in front of the porch.

"Who's first?" asks one peasant policeman, removing his homespun shirt and spreading it out on the ground; the crowd parts, because at this time one of the two holdouts (the dark-browed one) thrusts one of his shoulders forward, opens his eyes wide, and brandishes his beard with hostility; one small chosen peasant holds him by the sleeve. At the same time two men fly at the dark-browed peasant and try to topple him; but he waves his arms around desperately and falls on his knees in front of the old men, shaking his head wildly and saying with a choking voice: "Fathers! Dear ones! Benefactors! Elders!"

Behind him, tearfully regarding the old men and grasping his belt with his hand, stands the other holdout.

"Lay him down," says the elder quietly. . . .

The dark-browed peasant begins thrashing about, but several men fall on him and surround him; the crowd parts in the middle and then nosily crowds around him. "Elders," he moans for the last time, but now softly, as if from under the ground; the crowd recoils, there is the sound of a whip cracking, and after that, the man's terrible wild scream resounds. . . .

Mar'ia Nikolavna shrieks in horror, grabs her head, and runs away from the wattle fence. She races along the street without looking back, covering her ears; she runs past the church, knocking over people she meets, without seeing anything, until she reaches her house, rushes into her room, falls on her bed, and bursts into sobs. Shchetinin goes in to her. "What's the matter?" What happened?"

She waves her arm: "Go away! Everyone go away!"

CHAPTER XIII

––

MAR'IA NIKOLAVNA DIDN'T LEAVE HER ROOM THE whole day; Shchetinin spent it wringing his hands; at last he had the table set and had Riazanov summoned to dinner, while he himself paced the room in agitation; but he couldn't restrain himself—he went to find him in the annex, but met him on the stairs, took him by the arm, and led him into the hall. Entering the room, he glanced at the door and, getting tangled in his words, he said: "Listen! You know that we have a . . . difference of opinions, but that doesn't mean anything. . . . I believe you. Do you hear me?"

"Well, I do."

"I know that . . . you won't deceive me. . . . My situation is. . . . You understand, getting into my situation, how important it is for me to know the cause of what's going on here. I'm sure you'll explain it all to me. And in doing so, you'll demonstrate your . . . friendship."

"I can do that."

"Do me a favor, explain what happened to her. What's the cause?"

"The cause is very simple," Riazanov replied calmly. "She saw a peasant being flogged!"

"Nothing more?"

"Nothing more."

"Your word of honor?"

"You strange man! You yourself said that you believe me."

"Yes!"

Shchetinin slapped his forehead. "Let's go have dinner," he added with a sigh. "I was stupidly imagining. . . . However, you, my friend, are a fine fellow," he said merrily, sitting down at the table. "Why did you let her witness such corporal punishment?"

"What do you mean?"

"Why didn't you lead her away?"

"Why?"

"But you must agree, that . . . such a scene could shock anyone."

"So what?"

"But you were with her."

"What are you thinking? Were you hoping that in such a case I'd treat your wife the way cautious mothers treat their inexperienced daughters; that is, hand them a little book and say: 'Here you are, my dear, you can read this, but not what's hidden behind my finger.' So, I tell you, my dear friend, that in the first place, I never took that upon myself, and in the second place, you can't hide that sort of thing."

"Well let's suppose it may be just as you say, only . . . yes, as you like, inappropriate in the end."

"Ah! Well, that's your own business. You made a mistake when you didn't suggest that it was inappropriate for a proper lady to look at peasants when they're being flogged."

Several times during the course of that day Shchetinin crept up to his wife's room and put his ear to the door; not hearing anything, he declared to the servant that his wife was still asleep and had asked not to be disturbed. That evening he was planning to take care of some business, but was unable to do so: he rifled through his papers, moved some beads on his abacus, picked up a book, read for a while. . . . No, he was unable to read; he began adjusting the lamp: he kept turning it, but all that happened was that he smoked up the whole room; finally he put it out, lit a candle, chose several issues of the newspaper, and, walking very carefully, went into the hall. The windows there had been closed all day and therefore it was as stuffy as a bathhouse and it smelled of something odd, not exactly like paint, but like some military school. Shchetinin opened the windows, sat down at the table, and remained there a long time, with a newspaper on his lap, examining his own hall and constantly listening for something.

Late that evening, around eleven o'clock, Ivan Stepanych entered.

"Quiet, be quiet," Shchetinin whispered to him and motioned with his arm. "What is it?"

"Lend me your rifle."

Shchetinin was surprised. "What for?"

"What, sir?"

"Why do you want my rifle?"

"For the dog, sir. A mad dog's wandering around the village; it has to be shot."

"How will you shoot it now? It's dark."

"Early tomorrow morning. And lend me the newspapers after you've read them. I'd very much like to know more about those shorthaired girls. Did you read how skillfully they censured them? It was one mother. She says about herself: 'I,' she says, 'am a mother.' It's a very delightful article. You should read it!"

Shchetinin made no reply; after a little silence, he asked: "Listen, who was the one punished earlier today by the local office, do you know?"

"I don't, sir."

"It's so foolish, though," Shchetinin continued. "The devil knows what's going on! You ought to tell them; ask them why they do it. Is there really no other place, except out there on the street?"

"That's nothing," replied Ivan Stepanych with a laugh, "when I was living at the police superintendent's, Pëtr Ivanych, we used to flog them—flog them dreadfully! That was a real flogging. Afterward, he'd go out on the porch, light up his pipe. . . ."

"Well, yes; I know, I know," Shchetinin interrupted him.

"What, sir?"

"I've heard it. So, take the rifle; it's over there, in Agaf'ia's pantry. . . . But please, be quiet. Mar'ia Nikolavna's sleeping."

Carrying the rifle, Ivan Stepanych went to Riazanov's room and found him at his desk.

"What is it you're doing, writing something?"

"Yes, I am."

"Well, write away! I'm going to arrange quite the thing!"

"What?"

"I want to set up a village guard with some peasant lads."

"What for?"

"To destroy mad dogs. I've already rounded up about twenty of them, these lads; I've ordered them all to grab some sticks. Their sticks have spikes on them, very suitable. I'm teaching them. What fun! I'm teaching. You know what I'm calling them? *'Gminy.'*[1] 'Hey, you, *gmina*! And who am I?' 'Ivan Stepanych.' Then I grab him by his hair for daring to call me Ivan Stepanych. 'Who am I? I'm the *sołtys*.*[2] Who am I?' 'The *sołtys*.' 'That's right; good lad, give him some sugar.' Ha, ha, ha! What a job I have on my hands with these lads, I tell you. Goodbye!"

After sitting there until about two in the morning, Shchetinin fell asleep on the sofa in his study, without having undressed; the next morning he awoke late. The sky was overcast, and a light, almost invisible rain was falling; cold, clammy dampness was stealing through the windows. Shchetinin rubbed his eyes, looked around, and wanted to stretch out, when all of sudden he caught sight of a sealed letter on his desk. He picked it up, turned it over, shrugged his shoulders, and opened it. This is what it contained:

"I'm leaving. Don't try to dissuade me, because it won't do any good: I've been thinking it over for a long time; I've made my decision and now I know what I must do. Now I can say that *I don't love*

---

1. Polish term for a small rural administrative unit.
2. Polish term for the head of a larger administrative unit.

you; it's not only you, but in general it's everything that's occurring here, all these people . . . I hate them; I find all this repulsive. I fell out of love with you because you (consciously or not, it's all the same) compelled me to play a stupid role in your stupid comedy. For a long time I've been pondering all this, but yesterday one incident demonstrated to me conclusively in what a vile affair you've forced me to take an unwilling part. Naturally, you won't understand this; so much the worse for you. After all this I can't go on living here and don't want to, and besides . . . yes, in a word, I don't want to. Please, we'll have no further discussion of all this. . . ."

After reading through the letter, Shchetinin stood for several minutes in the middle of his room with his mouth half-open, holding his head with one hand, then rushed to Mar'ia Nikolavna's room—the door was locked. He knocked and asked permission to enter; he was told, "No." After standing at the door for a while, he left and wrote a note in which he repeated his request to discuss a very important matter; after a few minutes he received an answer written on the bottom of the same note: "Afterward."

He rumpled it up and, shoving it together with his hand into his pocket, stood in the middle of the room, thought a bit, and then went to the annex to see Riazanov; he turned out not to be there. Shchetinin went into the courtyard and set off without his hat, staring down at the ground, straight, past the stable, past the garden, across the road, along the boundary line, into the meadow. . . . The rain had begun to soak him; he kept walking, without looking back, without raising his eyes. He kept on walking and came to some sort of apiary. He stopped there, sat down on the grass, took his hand with the crumpled note from his pocket, unfolded it, and suddenly fell facedown on the ground and burst into tears like a child, rocking back and forth on the grass and filling the lonely apiary with his insane sobbing.

CHAPTER XIV

A NASTY GRAY DAY WAS ALMOST UNNOTICEABLY turning into twilight; a light frost was felt in the air. Riazanov, trousers tucked in his boots and hands clasped behind his back, was strolling along a narrow wooded path not far from the village. Next to him walked a young lad aged about seventeen (the deacon's son), barefoot, and wearing a white canvas coat—he was carrying his boots and a fishing pole over his shoulder; in his other hand he was holding some carp on a line; a large pointer with brown ears and clumsy, chubby paws ran ahead, roving eagerly from side to side. He would rush incessantly into the bushes, but would come back right away, apparently to show his thick-lipped snout; thumping the deacon's son's legs with his long, undocked tail, he would vanish again immediately. The path on which they walked skirted by various twists and turns the edge of a ravine thickly overgrown with hazelnuts and small oak trees; it led them into the depth of a copse, into impenetrable shrubbery, where they were suddenly enveloped by large drops of dew falling from leaves and where they had to bend over and make their way through a damp thicket and break some branches along their way; then this path led them to an opening at the very edge of a steep ravine, here overgrown by short, slippery grass, pitted by sheets of rain and strewn with small rocks. Before them opened a vista of fields shrouded in gray mist and meadows with blue lakes. Below, under the ravine, dark clusters of peasant huts could be glimpsed.

The deacon's son kept walking without looking down, without glancing from side to side, and only at the last moment pushed away the branches above him. He was very rapidly and anxiously explaining something to Riazanov, gesturing as he spoke with the hand in which he was holding his fish: "No, I still want to try one way," he was saying, after some thought.

"Which one? Persuasion again?"

"What else can I do, Iakov Vasil'ich? I have no other means."

"You've been trying to persuade him all summer, but he's not yielding at all. What did he tell you yesterday?"

"The same thing. The usual conversation: 'You,' he says, 'you're an unlucky ass. We have to marry you off,' he says, 'and there's nothing more to be discussed with you.'"

"And you still think he can be persuaded and will let you attend university? I'm eager to know how you plan to persuade him?"

"I found a passage in a book I have here. . . ."

"Yes?"

"It judiciously develops the argument that parents themselves become the obstacle on their children's path and deprive them of happiness."

"And what follows from this?"

"There are even several examples."

"That's all nonsense. No persuasion, no examples exist for parents. You attribute meaning to books, but for your father—that's all rubbish, written by loafers just like you; that's what happens, so there's no sense in talking about books!"

The deacon's son became thoughtful. "In that case, why did he provide me with the opportunity to develop?"

"He never did. He afforded you the chance to become a priest, to serve Christ, to perform rites. As a father, he wishes for your happiness in a form that, in his opinion, is available to you."

"What sort of father is he to me? He's my enemy, nothing more," said the young man, resentfully breaking off a branch blocking his way.

"If he's an enemy, then treat him accordingly! What use is persuasion? What you need is some intrigue, warlike cunning, if it's come to that. What are you waiting for?"

"There's nothing I can do alone here, Iakov Vasil'ich. But if. . . ."

"What?"

"If you were to help me, it would be an entirely different matter. What can I do alone?"

Riazanov was silent and scratched the back of his head; the deacon's son looked him in the eye and waited.

"All right. Let's go," said Riazanov.

The deacon's son gave a cheerful whistle; the pup immediately emerged from behind the bushes and all three of them started their descent into the ravine.

An hour later Riazanov returned home, tired and covered in mud up to his knees. After crossing the courtyard, he turned in to the kitchen and asked for the samovar for some tea.

When he arrived back at the annex, it was already twilight; his room was dark and smelled of the damp; trees were rustling in the garden and there was a muffled sound of raindrops dropping from the leaves against his windows. Riazanov lit a candle and, without removing his cap, stood in the middle of the room, thoughtfully observing its walls, and the rough woodwork of the bed and table covered with books and pieces of paper. His own shadow, cast on the partition overlaid with old newspapers, remained motionless, his head bent back to the ceiling; behind the partition the siskin shuddered half-asleep and rustled its wings in its new cage.

After standing there several minutes, Riazanov took off his wet clothes and put on his warm coat; hunching up, he sat down at the table. The paper lying on the table in front of him was covered with diminutive, undecipherable writing and stained with ink. He opened a new issue of a journal, searched through his papers, found a notebook with rough drafts, and for a long time checked it against the journal, stroking his beard with one hand, tracing the lines with his other hand; then he closed the journal and the notebook, tossed it onto the window sill, and sank into thought. The footman entered carrying things for tea on a tray; just as Riazanov was starting to pour the tea, he heard the rustling of a woman's dress from behind the partition.

"Aren't you feeling well?" Mar'ia Nikolavna asked with an anxious look as she entered the room.

"No, it's nothing; I caught a little chill. It's damp. I was in the woods, and, well, I got soaked."

"Aren't you ashamed for not taking better care of yourself?" she said, shaking her head. "Would you like some raspberry jam? Wait, I'll do it. Give it to me; you don't know how. Would you like to have some heat in here? Hmm, I'll tell them right away."

"There's no need to concern yourself! I'll drink some hot tea and it'll pass."

"Well, yes. Of course! It'll pass just like that! It's no joking matter."

"You really seem to think I'm ill. Why have you come here?"

Mar'ia Nikolavna glanced around. "What do you mean? Am I disturbing you?"

"No, I said it because you've gone out in the damp and your feet will get wet."

"What do you care about my feet? That's very sweet. Perhaps I intentionally want to get them wet; perhaps I want to die."

"Really? Well. . . ."

"Well what?"

Riazanov smiled. "You're an amusing woman," he said, fastening all the buttons on his coat and sitting down at the table.

Mar'ia Nikolavna also sat down, poured him a glass of tea with raspberry jam, and placed a decanter with rum in front of him.

"If I were to die, there's no one to weep over me," she said folding her hands in her lap.

Riazanov glanced at her from under his brows and made no reply; then he picked up the decanter, poured himself some rum, and said: "What about Aleksandr Vasil'ich?"

Mar'ia Nikolavna made a dismissive gesture with her arm. "That doesn't matter to me."

Riazanov added some sugar to his glass, stirred it, and asked: "But might it matter to others?"

"Of course."

"In other words, that's not what you want to say. People will weep, but not the right ones; you're afraid that in the event of your death, disorder might result. Is that it?"

"Well, yes. But what a foolish conversation I've begun, about death and various other things. . . . God knows what!"

"Why is it foolish? No, not at all; it's appropriate: dusk, nasty weather; it's the right time to talk about death."

She shook her head in silence; Riazanov waited a bit to see what she'd say and then took a big sip from his glass. Just then, somewhere beyond the garden, a rifle shot rang out. Mar'ia Nikolavna shuddered. "What's that?" she asked in alarm.

"That must be Ivan Stepanych amusing himself."

She thought a bit; glancing around apprehensively, she said: "No, I don't want to die, I don't."

"Nobody's forcing you to."

"Let's . . . let's talk about something else instead, something good. Do you know why I've come to see you?"

"Well?"

"I want to talk with you about a very important matter."

"What is it?"

"First of all, I want to say something about you."

"Me? Well, that subject's not too interesting."

"On the contrary, to me it's very interesting, all the more so since it's connected to various other matters."

"Yes. So what would you like from me?"

"In the first place, I'd like it if you wouldn't talk to me that way."

"What way?"

"Using that tone. I very much like it when you use that tone with others, but not with me."

"But that tone . . . how can I say it? It's the kind of thing that doesn't depend only on my desire."

"On what then?"

"It depends more, I suppose, on the life that surrounds us."

"You mean to say there are dissonances in this life."

"No, I mean to say that the tone's set by life and we merely pick it up. Perhaps we could raise it a bit, but what's the sense in that? Life will force it back."

"So you think," said Mar'ia Nikolavna after some thought, "that in this life"—she gestured with her hand all around—"there's nothing that would compel you to speak in even a little different way from the way you do. All right. Let's assume that's the case. Well, and what about earlier? Is it really true that in your life there have never been any cases or some events that angered you or made you feel ecstatic? Well? Have there been?"

"Of course there were; what of it?"

"So, and now? Right here? Well, what are you thinking right now, at this very minute? About your situation, for example, what do you think? Tell me!"

"My situation? What's there to think? In general I'm now living in a summer situation, in the country, and am spending my time pleasantly; I thought I caught a little cold, but now I've drunk some raspberry tea and begun to perspire; furthermore, I think that a woman is sitting here with me, a fine woman, and we're engaging in idle chatter about this and that. That's all."

"No, you haven't understood me correctly."

"Very possibly."

"I want to know how you regard everything that surrounds you here in the country, everything that occurs here. Can it be that since you've arrived here nothing's happened that could strike you, surprise you, make you glad or make you sad?"

"I really don't recall. That must mean there wasn't anything.

And I don't know what you find strange about this. If you'd think for a bit, you'd be convinced that there was nothing special of that kind. Life is life: everything's done in strict conformity and to the proper order; there aren't any accidents and can't be any. Why be made glad or sad? In Koshansky's *Rhetoric*, there's the following example (God only knows how it wound up there):[1] 'Here,' he says, 'the bear throttles a wolf, the wolf kills a sheep, the sheep eats the grass, the grass receives sustenance from the earth; and the lion,' he says, 'conquers the bear and the wolf and the sheep and everything else.' That's the order of things. Now, what sort of accidents can exist? Can it happen that when the wolf's killing a sheep, he doesn't finish the job because at that very moment the bear starts to throttle him, or that the lion ambles past the bear and doesn't disturb him? Such contingencies happen—that's for sure; but I see no reason to be surprised by them."

"I understand all that. But why, when you talk about these matters, does it seem as if you think all this must be so? Of course, I don't believe that."

"That's too bad."

"What do you mean, too bad? Are you saying that intentionally, for them?"

"On the contrary, I'm saying it for them and for you, and I say just what I think to everyone."

"Accordingly, you think that all these atrocities must happen?"

"What atrocities?"

"Why, those that . . . well, I don't know. . . . In a word, this entire household . . . the fact that the peasants have to be punished, that they're to be paid as little as possible for their work, and so on."

"I never said that all this was necessary and couldn't be otherwise."

"But you think it's all very natural and normal."

1. Nikolai F. Koshansky (1784 or 1785–1831) was a well-known scholar of classical languages and literatures and a devoted teacher; his most important work, *Obshchaia ritorika* [*General Rhetoric*] was published posthumously in 1832.

"Don't you agree? That's only because you don't want to think. Let's suppose you put a man into a smoky room and charcoal fumes poison him—would that, in your opinion, be unnatural? If he's deprived of food for two full days and his stomach feels pinched with hunger, would that, in your opinion, be unnatural?"

"Well, of course it would; only you'll agree that it's not a natural desire to starve another person?"

"I can't agree with that at all, because if only one portion of bread is issued to two people, and of those two, one is stronger than the other, then from the point of view of the stronger, the most natural outcome would be to take the bread away from the weaker person. What could be more natural than this motivation? And that, however, in no way interferes with a person's ability in another case to deprive himself of food in favor of another, that is, to follow a completely contradictory motivation, which, in turn, is also very natural and normal. Everything depends on the circumstances in which a person is placed: in some circumstances he'll strangle and rob a close relative; in others, he'll take off and give away the shirt on his back. The visible results are always natural and normal, once the cause is known; but that's not the point."

"Then what is?"

"It's what you and I don't see and don't know. There's an unknown quantity; that's the whole point and it's all . . . it's all not worth a damn."

Riazanov fell silent and downed his glass of cold raspberry tea. "You ask," he began again, "you ask why I'm not horrified, why I don't rejoice, why I'm not surprised at what I see here. All right. But what do I see here? What sort of pictures could be here that would be worthy of astonishment? Well, first of all I see a diligent peasant; I see that he digs the earth and earns his bread by the sweat of his brow; then I observe that at a certain distance from him stand some people I've recently met and they're patiently waiting while the diligent landowner enjoys the work and produces a yield; then they'll approach this peasant and, in the most polite manner, take from him all that they can according to the rules for the good of enlightenment, and they'll leave him with only as much as he needs for his own use to maintain 'the form of a slave' and not perish from starvation.[2] That's picture number one. What can surprise me here, I ask you? The peasant's diligence? But that's why, in fact, he's called diligent; that quality was ascribed to him long ago; he's even called that in Latin: *sedulus rusticus*—diligent peasant; therefore, there's no more to be said. Now it's already too late: like it or not, be diligent because that's the reputation he's earned. And there's nothing to be surprised about. What else is there? The generosity of my acquaintances? But if they weren't generous and if they were to take everything away from him at once, they'd be depriving him of the opportunity to enjoy his labor in the future, they'd be starving him to death, and then who would be left to work for the good of enlightenment? Therefore, they have to appear generous; hence, there's little that is surprising. Necessity! That's all there is to it. And I hope you aren't surprised either. No? Splendid. What else do I see here? I see others of my acquaintance, sitting by the waters of Babylon, sitting and weeping, wiping away bitter tears with redemption certificates.[3] That's picture number two. But the reason for their sorrow, probably, is well known to you, too: once again, need, once more, necessity; therefore, even here . . . but no, do you know," said Riazanov, growing more animated, "do you know that this entire mechanism is so simple that one must really be surprised that there're still people on earth who rack their brains over such nonsense, who don't understand, who're surprised. . . . Why, after this, then what? Afterward one must be surprised that I drank a sudorific[4] and suddenly began sweating. Isn't that strange, don't you think?"

2. This phrase is most likely from the New Testament, Apostle Paul's *Letter to the Philippians* 2:5–7, which incorporates the words of an old Christian hymn: "Take to heart among yourselves what you find in Christ Jesus: 'He was in the form of God; yet he laid no claim to equality with God, but made himself nothing, assuming the form of a slave. . . .'"
3. A partial quotation from the Hebrew Bible, Psalm 137:1: "By the waters of Babylon, there we sat down and wept, when we remembered Zion."
4. A medicine used to induce perspiration.

"That's all true, let's assume. But don't you agree that it's impossible to regard this all hardheartedly, impossible not to lament that all this is true?"

"What's the sense of this lamentation? I know many people who lament the fact that our nation is so great, so valiant, that it has so much strength, hope, and so forth, and all of it, one can say, goes for naught. Excellent. It's just as if I were to go into the forest, stand in front of an oak tree, and say: 'Oh, my God! Such a splendid tree and the poor thing's so soiled by birds and gnawed by worms, and by the way, pigs are making use of it for their victuals; and if that very same oak tree were to be in good hands, what sort of benefit could it accomplish? How many sleigh runners could come from it, let alone wooden tubs, barrels, buckets, and other useful household utensils? And the wooden parquet from it, perhaps, would be exceptional.' Well? What do you think, is this lamentable or not?"

"Well, yes. I understand. It means there's nothing to be done here."

"No, it means merely that there's a certain point of view from which the most curious affair seems so simple and clear that it's tedious to consider. You wanted to know my view of things; well, it's at your service. But usually people don't like it and, as if intentionally, choose such matters that would stump the devil himself, because although little good could come of it, on the other hand at every step one can be surprised, delighted, or horrified. Well, meanwhile time's passing, and it seems as if you're really living."

Mar'ia Nikolavna became pensive. "Yes, that's true," she said at last, "it's better to live somehow, even foolishly, but to live, rather than. . . ."

"However, this life here no longer pleases you. Why is that? You've come to understand its absurdity and can no longer live it. Therefore, the more you learn about life in general, the more you'll be deprived of the possibility of living the way everyone else does."

"But then what?" Mar'ia Nikolavna asked almost in horror. "What's left for a person to do who's lost the possibility of living life the way other people do?"

"It follows," Riazanov said, looking around, "it follows that one must conceive, invent a new life, and until then. . . ." He waved his arm contemptuously.

"No, wait! Tell me: after all, you do have a life that you live?"

"Of course I do."

"Well, I'd like to know about it. What sort of life is it?"

"You're wasting your time. It's not worth knowing."

"Why not?"

"Because it's not a life: the devil knows what it is. It's some sort of nonsense, like all the others."

She paused. "No, that can't be so."

Riazanov shrugged his shoulders.

"I don't believe you. It's just that you don't want to tell me."

"You must understand: there's nothing to say."

"Is it that I'm not worth telling? Listen," she began suddenly, extending her hand to him. "Would you like to be my friend? Well? Would you?"

Without looking her in the face, he silently squeezed her hand, then carefully released his hand and placed hers on the table.

Mar'ia Nikolavna, leaning slightly toward him, waited for him to speak.

"Yes," he said at last, "that's very nice, of course, but. . . ."

"What?"

"I really don't understand what sort of friendship could exist between us," he concluded softly, as if talking to himself. "Nothing would come of it."

"But if you don't understand," she added rapidly, "I tell you that I'm leaving here."

"What? How? Completely?"

"Yes, completely. Everything's over and done with between my husband and me. I'm free."

"Aha," Riazanov said quietly, staring at the floor.

"Now I'd like just one thing," said Mar'ia Nikolavna, becoming more and more animated. "I'd like to arrange my life so I can use all my strength, all my abilities to be useful to you in some way. I don't want a lot; I'd merely like to assist you a little in your endeavor. I'll do whatever you tell me. At first, of course, I'll need your help because I don't know how to do anything; but then I'll gradually get used to it. This way, we'll help each other. . . ."

"In what?"

"What do you mean?"

"Have you thought about how we'd help each other? I don't quite understand what sort of endeavor you've found. Will we learn from each other or simply live? But no, wait! First of all, here's what: why exactly are you leaving?"

"You still don't know?"

"No, I don't."

"All right. I'll tell you. I'm leaving to begin a new, completely new life—this one's become repulsive to me; these people are so revolting, as is this entire country life. I could remain here only so long as I was still waiting for something, in a word, when I still believed: now I see that I've nothing to wait for, that one can merely make money here, and even that, only through someone else's labor. I feel loathing for landowners and all those proprietors; I despise them; I feel sorry for the peasants, of course, but what can I do? I don't have the strength to help them, nor do I want to look at them and just sob my eyes out. That's unbearable. Well, now tell me, isn't all this true? There's no reason for me to stay here any longer, is there? Right?"

"Yes, of course, if you really find it all so revolting."

"You're just saying that. . . . It seems to me that you don't want me to leave."

"It seems like that for no reason. On the contrary, I want you to do whatever you want to; but, in addition, I'd still like to hear an answer to the question I posed: why do you want to go *there?*" He pointed to the window. "What draws you *dahin, dahin?*[5] Do you seriously think that lemons grow there?"

"Do you know, in fact, how I envision what's *there?* I've always imagined that somewhere live such fine people, so clever and kind, who know everything, tell everything, teach what to do and how to do it, who assist and shelter anyone who comes to them . . . in a word, good people, very good people. . . ."

"Yes," Riazanov said in deep thought. "Good people. . . . Yes, there were such people. It's true."

"And now?"

"Now, maybe only five or so can be found."

"What? Why so few? Where are they?"

"Hmm. You ask strange questions! Aren't they people, too? Aren't they prone to various human weaknesses? Some of them die, and others don't. . . ."

"So then?"

"They merely perish. . . ."

"How?"

"Just so, they disappear—and that's that. It's just like the ballet: they keep dancing and dancing, they find their place—and all of a sudden, bang! They disappear."

Mar'ia Nikolavna sighed and became pensive.

"Yes, they've winnowed out those who are stronger, winnowed them all out," Riazanov continued in the meantime, "and only the small fry are left. However, pay no attention to the fact that they're small fry. There's no need. This group of small fry can cope with all the tasks and organize all the artels[6] . . . on a legal foundation; they'll shelter you and explain their

---

5. "Whither, whither?" [Ger.] from Mignon's Song in Goethe's novel, *Wilhelm Meister's Apprenticeship* (1795), which opens with one of the most famous lines in German poetry, an allusion to Italy: "*Kennst du das Land, wo die Zitronen blühn?*" ("Do you know the land where the lemon trees bloom?").

6. Cooperative associations of workers or peasants that existed in the Russian Empire beginning in the 1860s.

ways to you, the how and the what . . . yes, but you'll see for yourself."[7]

"And you?" Mar'ia Nikolavna asked with surprise.

"No, I'll have to do without this, by my own means."

"But why? Don't you believe in the success of this endeavor?"

"Of course, I do. It's impossible not to believe. Success will undoubtedly come, but we, it seems that we . . . we came a little late to enjoy this success."

Riazanov slowly surveyed the room with his eyes; leaning back in his chair, he ran his hand over his hair. Mar'ia Nikolavna attentively followed every one of his words, while staring him in the eye without blinking.

"Yes," he began again, "life's a curious thing, I tell you. You see through it all, it seems, and you get to know a person inside out; what more can there be? But no, it's still too little. There's something more you need. Passion is necessary. One must simply come and take it. . . . But I'm talking and talking while sipping this raspberry tea; I completely forgot that there's rum in it, damn it! I'm drunk." He pushed away his glass. "That's how I realized, somehow I began to . . . express myself in a very flowery manner," he added, sitting up straight in the chair.

And in fact, crimson blotches were appearing on his face and his eyes shifted uneasily and suspiciously from one object to another. He stood up and took a few steps around the room, obviously trying to move as steadily as he could.

"I was about to ask you one more thing," Mar'ia Nikolavna said hesitantly.

"What's that?" Riazanov turned around, thrust his hands in his pockets, and stopped in front of Mar'ia Nikolavna.

"Go on, ask it! I only drank so much because of the damp weather."

---

7. This revolutionary enthusiasm echoes that of N. G. Chernyshevsky's "New People" in his most controversial and influential novel, *What Is to Be Done?* (1863).

"Never mind."

"But it seems you even wanted to see me in an abnormal state: so here's a splendid instance."

Mar'ia Nikolavna raised her head and looked him in the eye.

"What are you looking at? Do you think I'll be more open? No, alcohol has the completely opposite effect on me: I become even more distrustful and discourteous. Yet it seems that even when I was completely sober I didn't treat you very tactfully. Well? Mar'ia Nikolavna! Isn't that so? Did I behave rudely to you? Don't be angry for it! It's mere trifles. . . ." He swayed.

"Sit down," she said softly, taking him by the hand.

"Well, then, what was it you wanted to ask me?" he said, sitting back down at his previous place.

"You still haven't told me. . . . You haven't said anything at all about . . ." she hesitated and bent down further toward the table; then speaking slowly and deliberately, almost in a whisper, she added, "Can it be that you still don't know?"

"I know only one thing," Riazanov said, interrupting her, "and I know it in the most definitive way: that tomorrow I'm leaving here."

"Where to?" Mar'ia Nikolavna asked, raising her head quickly.

"That depends on . . . in general, to various places."

Mar'ia Nikolavna didn't take her eyes off him and was waiting for something more.

"More to the south," Riazanov added.

She didn't move, didn't even wince, and continued staring at him as before, although from her eyes it was obvious that she was no longer expecting anything; her thoughts had taken flight.

"Bad weather's coming," Riazanov continued, looking out the window. "It's going to rain. You see, the weather's filthy!"

Mar'ia Nikolavna kept looking at him and probably not listening; her glance moved from Riazanov to the wall and it stayed there; her face expressed nothing; it was completely motionless and suddenly looked drawn, as if after a serious illness. Riazanov was silent and began staring at her intently. Frowning slightly, he cast his eyes over her whole face, over her hands, open on the table and lying there still, while at the same time he decisively and without haste rubbed his hands so hard that his knuckles cracked; then he wanted to take a deep breath; he inhaled, but immediately bit his lip and managed to stifle his breath; then he stood up and brushed against the leg of the table.

"Well?" Mar'ia Nikolavna asked anxiously, suddenly coming back to her senses.

Riazanov silently picked up a book from the windowsill.

She ran her hand over her face, looked around, and treading on her own dress—noticing nothing—was about to take several steps toward the door; but then paused and turned around. Riazanov stood, head bowed, near the window, a book in his hand. Mar'ia Nikolavna glanced at him and said in an cold, flat tone of voice: "Farewell!"

"Where will you go?" he asked softly.

"I'll go . . . now I'm going home, but afterward I'll go. . . ."

"There?"

"Yes, there," she said firmly and headed for the door.

"I wish you success," he said without stirring from his place as she was leaving the room; almost at the same moment he hurled the book with all his might under the table; seizing his hair with both hands, he rushed forward . . . but then stopped, dropped his hands, shook his head, smiled, and began pacing the room.

CHAPTER XV

—

IT RAINED THAT NIGHT AND TOWARD MORNING THE weather had taken a real turn for the worse: the sky was completely clouded over and the road was slushy.

Shchetinin was sitting on the sofa in his study, his legs tucked up under him, and staring pensively out the window. Of late he had changed considerably and grown thinner; he'd become noticeably sloppy in his attire: he didn't have a tie on and was wearing an old, tattered jacket and a pair of slippers. A book was sprawling on the sofa next to him; Ivan Stepanych sat at the desk and was finishing up some paper; the sounds of a peasant's cough could be heard, and the hasty tramping of dirty boots, in the entrance hall. Shchetinin was trying to read the book; he held it in his hands, looked at it, even licked his finger to turn the page, but then he fell into thought again and began staring out the window, although, to tell the truth, there was really nothing to look at: some wet folks were waddling across the bricks in the courtyard; sparrows were sitting on the rooftops, huddled up, shaking their wet wings gloomily.

"I've finished, sir," Ivan Stepanych said abruptly, laying a pen down on the table. "Sign it, if you please!"

Shchetinin reluctantly stood up from the sofa, picked up the pen lethargically, and signed with a single stroke: "Landowner, Collegiate Secretary Aleksandr Vasil'ich Shchetinin,"[1] and sat back down on the sofa.

"I've earmarked that hide to be worked on," Ivan Stepanych said, sprinkling sand over the signature.

"Aha," Shchetinin said indifferently.

"I want to have a hat made, of dog's fur. Skunk would also be perfect. The one I shot."

"Hmm."

"No, I want to ask you something," Ivan Stepanych said, getting up. "Aleksandr Vasil'ich!"

"What?"

"Do you know science?"

"I do."

"I want to ask you if it's true or not."

"If what's true?"

"It was rabid."

"If who was?"

"About that hat. It was made from a rabid dog."

"Well, so what?"

"I heard that if, they say, you bring the hat close to water, then the fur on it would stand up on end. Have you read that in any of your books?"

"No, I haven't."

Ivan Stepanych grew pensive. "Perhaps they're lying. I don't give a damn; I'll still make the hat," he decided, waving the paper. "And there might even be enough for a collar on my overcoat. Well? It was a huge, ferocious dog. What do you think? Will there be enough?

1. Shchetinin's official designation in the Table of Ranks, a formal list of positions and ranks in the military, government, and court of Imperial Russia, introduced by Peter the Great in 1722.

It's this big!" He indicated its size with his hands. "Yes, it will. I know it will," said Ivan Stepanych, standing in front of Shchetinin. "There's only one thing that's bad," he said, shaking his head.

"What's that?" Shchetinin asked, coming back to his senses.

"They say you can't enter a church wearing this overcoat."

"Why not?"

"Because the collar's made from dog fur."

"Well, never mind," said Shchetinin. "Here's what: give this paper to the peasants and talk to them about our business."

"Hey, I'm fed up with those discussions," said Ivan Stepanych with dissatisfaction and headed into the entrance hall. A minute later one could hear the sound of swearing coming from there.

Shchetinin became pensive again. Just then Riazanov came in. His face reflected a desire to appear as apathetic as possible, and therefore he seemed somehow too unconcerned. Shchetinin, noticing him from afar, was about to frown, but looking him in the eye, asked: "So, I heard you weren't feeling well?"

"No. I've come to say farewell," replied Riazanov, sitting down next to him on the sofa. "I'm leaving."

"What? Already?" Shchetinin stood up. "Together?"

"I'm going alone," Riazanov replied clearly.

Shchetinin lowered himself onto the sofa again. "When?" he asked, taking a breath.

"As soon as they bring the horses around. I've sent for them."

Shchetinin picked at the pillow in silence. "Why do you want to travel in such bad weather?" he asked at last with feigned sympathy.

"One way or another I'll get wet: if not today, then tomorrow. What difference does it make?"

"Well, take the covered carriage, at least as far as town."

"Don't be ridiculous! That's foolish." Riazanov waved his arm dismissively.

"Well, as you like. Where are you off to—Piter?"[2]

---

2. As mentioned in chapter I, an affectionate diminutive for of St. Petersburg.

"No, anyplace. That's not the point. Actually, I came to. . . ."

Shchetinin sighed again and, tucking his legs up under him, turned to Riazanov, trying, however, not to look him in the eye.

"Lately," Riazanov began, "some disagreements have arisen between us. Not that it matters to me, but it seems that you have reason to be dissatisfied with me, so I came to give you an account before my departure."

Shchetinin shrugged his shoulders. "To tell the truth, I don't know what sort of accounting we could have. Of course, however . . . I can only say one thing, that I never would've expected this of you."

"I think, on the other hand, one should always have expected it."

Shchetinin flared up in anger. "What is it you want from me in the end?" he shouted, jumping up from the sofa. "You've taken everything away from me: you robbed me of my energy, my serenity, and in addition, you've destroyed my family happiness. . . . In spite of all that, you consider it all foolish; in spite of all that, up to now I was living here, doing my work, well, foolish work in your opinion, but at least I know that I was laboring and not idling away my life . . . while here, with all these conversations . . . and in addition, you say I'm to blame for everything. That's very nice indeed!" Shchetinin was rushing around the room, waving his arms wildly.

"Who's blaming you? Calm down, do me a favor," said Riazanov, also getting up from the sofa. "Can someone really be to blame in this situation?"

"So then, in your opinion, it's just fate?"

"Fate or not, in any case it's an unknown. Sooner or later this had to happen."

"If it weren't for these conversations, nothing would've happened."

"What about the conversations? Do you think it was just the conversations, and Lord knows what else?"

"Absolutely! If every day from morning 'til night what's drummed in your ear is, 'This is wrong,' 'That isn't so. . . . ' She's a young woman, inexperienced: it's understandable that she fell for you. But you didn't fall for her?"

"Me? That's a completely different thing. That's the point. The power, my friend, is not in me. If it hadn't been with me, then it would've been with another man; if not with someone else, then with some woman with whom she was having a heart-to-heart; but the same thing would've happened. If not now, then in a year, but she'd have left anyway. You could always prohibit all conversation . . . but you'd have to take into account that there are books like that. She'd understand this whole business even without conversation. There's nothing you could do about it."

Shchetinin became pensive.

"It's no use trying to find someone to blame," added Riazanov. "I'd thought about all that already: there's no way out."

"But why is that, why?" Shchetinin asked, once again coming to life. "What did I ever do to her? There has to be some basis or other. I'm not a milksop, after all, just ordering me around: now I love, now I don't."

"The basis, my friend, is life itself. This woman wants to live; you and I are merely participating in this affair as gracious witnesses. Our roles are the most pointless: she needed you to be liberated from her mother; I liberated her from you; and she liberated herself from me. Now she doesn't need anyone—she's her own mistress."[3]

Shchetinin stood by the window and ran his fingers over the glass. "So then, you're not leaving with her?" he asked softly at last.

"I told you already, I'm going alone, and in a completely different direction."

"Hmm," Shchetinin said thoughtfully, "then that's an entirely different conversation."

"The conversation is very brief," Riazanov observed. "'May

---

3. These themes are explored in Chernyshevsky's *What Is to Be Done?*, especially in Vera Pavlovna's allegorical dreams.

the man asleep in his grave sleep on, and may the living live their lives!'"[4]

"So, should I just up and die?"

"Die or not, as you please, but you and I won't do much carousing at life's feast. Our places there have long been taken by others."

"No, friend, don't say that! I still want to live. I won't give up so easily. Family life may not have worked out for me; so, what can I do? I'll try something else. Life still lies ahead. After all, I'm only thirty years old. That's something!"

Riazanov was silent.

"But in the midst of my grief," Shchetinin continued, lowering his tone significantly, "I happened upon this little book, and with nothing better to do, I began looking through it. . . ."

"Yes."

"Not bad. It's a sensible book."

"Well, what does it say?"

"I find that the author's absolutely correct: he says that without capital no serious, solid undertaking is possible."

"Yes."

"And he says that first of all it's necessary to acquire large financial resources, and only then, when you have some money in hand, can you do what you want . . . make any revolutions you like. . . ."

"Yes. And what does this have to do with you?"

"It's that this book leads me to altogether new propositions; it's shown me that all is not yet lost. To tell you the truth, I'm not angry with you at all. You can't undo what's already been done. But I can't just sit here with my arms folded and weep over my fate; I have to do something; I need some occupation, and I've come up with one."

"How curious."

"Yes, my friend, there'll be a holiday in our neighborhood; and

4. The last two lines of the lyric poem "The Victory Festival" (1828) by V. A. Zhukovsky, a free translation of Friedrich Schiller's *"Das Siegesfest"* (1803), on the futility of military victories.

may God grant that it also serves the common good. Only give me time to grow rich and then with some money we'll accomplish all these deeds."

"God willing!"

Shchetinin had become almost cheerful: his rumpled face had grown lively; he'd begun pacing the room and, smiling at his own thoughts, he was stroking his own head; then all of a sudden, he stopped.

"Yes! What am I saying? You're leaving. I completely forgot. Do you want to have a bite to eat?"

"No, I don't."

"It's not possible, my friend. Although you and I are rivals in a certain sense," Shchetinin said jokingly, "we still have to celebrate the send-off appropriately; at least we can open and split a bottle." He ordered a bottle of wine.

"Well then, my friend," Shchetinin said, now completely cheered up, and slapping Riazanov's knee. "Autumn's coming, I'll buy up the grain, and in spring I'll raise sheep. The main thing is—to accumulate as much money as possible, and then. . . . Then I'll get to see what you say, I'll get to see."

"I can tell you now what I'll say."

"What's that?"

"You're singing an old song: 'I'll get rich and then I'll begin to benefit mankind.'"

"Well, even if it's an old song, what's so bad about that? I'm telling you how I'll put the money to good use."

"I understand. Let's assume your goal is a good one, but the means. . . ."

"How? Money is power."

"Power it is, of course, power; but here's what's wicked: while you're acquiring it, you'll manage to hurt mankind so badly that afterward all your wealth won't be enough to make amends. And the main thing is that it will be difficult to make amends: the desire to acquire leads to the habit. The result is that force will be needed to take the money away from you."

"Why do you constantly see evil everywhere and in everything? Can't I do it in an honest way?"

"Mmm—it's hard. Moreover, one of my acquaintances, an archdeacon, used to say that there was one instance in which a virtuous young lady preserved her innocence and acquired her capital. Yes, such cases do occur, but they're rare."

The footman brought in a bottle of Rhine wine on a tray with two glasses.

"Hearing you talk," Shchetinin said, pouring wine into the glasses, "the only thing left to do is to tie a large stone around my neck and throw myself into the water. Let's drink: that would be a better thing to do."

"Of course, it's better," observed Riazanov and clinked glasses with Shchetinin. "But will you really raise sheep?"

"I will, my friend; you'll have to forgive me for it!"

"Well, yes. And you'll still speculate in grain?"

"I will, friend: what's to be done? I will. It's impossible not to, because we engage in trade; it's wrong to sell at a loss."

"Of course. Don't listen to people! All sorts of things will be said, but you can't listen to it all. However, it's time for me to go. They've brought the horses around."

Shchetinin glanced out the window: in the courtyard, next to the annex, stood a cart harnessed with a pair of shaggy peasant horses; a peasant sat up on the box.

"By the way, where are you headed? Eh?" asked Shchetinin. "To what places?"

"Such things aren't known for sure," Riazanov replied with a smile. "Well, farewell!"

"Farewell, friend, farewell," Shchetinin said, somehow both pensively and drawlingly, shaking his hand. "Do you know what I want to say to you? You may or may not believe it; but so help me God, I feel sorry for you; that is, sincerely sorry. Word of honor."

"I believe it," Riazanov said softly and began wrapping his handkerchief around his neck.

"And for me to decide now to roam the wide world," Shchetinin said in the meantime, putting his hands in his pockets and swaying slightly, "that is, it seems, even if you shower me with gold so I'd agree—not me, not for anything in the world! Without shelter, without refuge, nothing behind, nothing ahead. . . ."

"Goodbye," Riazanov said abruptly and turned to leave. As he walked through the front entrance he saw Mar'ia Nikolavna in the hall; she was standing in the doorway, leaning against the post, apparently waiting for him. He went up to her.

"I wanted to bid you farewell," she said, moving away from the door and inviting him to enter the hall.

"I did, too," said Riazanov, removing his cap. He glanced at her face: it was perfectly calm, even a bit triumphant, and it reminded him of her expression three months ago when Riazanov had first arrived in the country.

"You and I," she began, "have talked so much all summer that. . . ."

"We've talked about everything," Riazanov prompted her.

"No, not everything," she observed drily. "Since you talked more than I did, and I merely listened, now it's your turn to listen to what I have to say."

"I'm listening," Riazanov said, inclining his head.

"I wanted . . . in the first place, to thank you for everything you've done for me, and in addition, for the conversation we had yesterday."

Riazanov stood in front of her, his head bowed, his eyes lowered, and he listened.

"I'm particularly grateful for that clarification." She stressed the word *particularly*. "With that clarification you kept me from making a very grave mistake. That night I experienced a spiritual crisis, but now I'm completely recovered. You helped me greatly. Perhaps you yourself were unaware of the service you rendered. But I must tell you one more thing, which probably will come as a big surprise to you. Listen! All our discussions, all of them, I recall beyond question; I've forgotten nothing; I remember every word you said and I know that it's all so and that you spoke the truth. . . ."

"Yes."

"But, it's strange—just think, today I don't believe you; that is, somehow I just don't believe you. Of course, that will surprise you."

"No," replied Riazanov, raising his eyes. "I know of a similar case when another lady said that to me: 'I know,' she said, 'that the world is round, but I don't believe it.'"

Mar'ia Nikolavna bit her lips and said hastily: "Well, yes, and I know you have sufficient cleverness, but your efforts are in vain; this time I'm being completely earnest."

"And this time I'm replying in earnest: there was nothing to offend you in the comparison I just made. On the contrary, it was perfectly appropriate: don't believe anyone, including even me; that way you'll have fewer spiritual crises and make fewer mistakes."

"No, I won't agree to that."

"In that case, it's just as you wish, but I must leave now because while we stand here chatting, the diligent peasant who's offered to conduct me as far as town is losing a great deal of valuable time."

"Ah, I won't keep you any longer."

"Do you have anything more to communicate to me?"

"Nothing."

Mar'ia Nikolavna shook her head. "Farewell!" She extended her hand. Riazanov glanced fleetingly once more at her face: it was completely cold.

"Farewell, Ivan Stepanych," said Riazanov as he entered the annex.

"You're leaving? Where to? Well, now! Don't go!"

"What's to be done? I have to leave."

"Hey, you! I'd been hoping to go rabbit hunting with you, huh? We'd have had a grand time! Well, wait a moment, I'll help you with your things," he said, taking the bundle from Riazanov's hands. "You can't do anything."

Riazanov had set about fastening his suitcase.

"Well then, really," said Ivan Stepanych, "I'll look around myself, have a look, and maybe I'll head off somewhere, too, to Poland," he suddenly decided, lifting the bundle. "Huh? What do you think? A fine thing! Are you going to Poland, too? Go! Go! There are quite some places to see there, I hear."[5]

"Yes, there are quite some places," Riazanov replied without listening, leaning over his suitcase.

While Riazanov was loading his belongings onto the cart with Ivan Stepanych's assistance, the deacon's elderly wife was approaching the annex and escorting her son, who was dressed in a rabbitskin coat. She repeatedly made the sign of the cross over him and helped him into the cart, bundling him up and covering him with an old cotton blanket; then she hastily retrieved from her bosom some small packets and, as if concealing them from someone, stealthily placed them in his pocket; at last she removed her own headscarf and wrapped it around his neck.

Mar'ia Nikolavna stood at the window the whole time and when the peasant tugged at the reins and took his switch to the horses, she sighed; lowering her head, she quietly and pensively returned to her own room and began packing her things for the journey.

---

5. A veiled reference to the January Uprising, a rebellion in the former Polish-Lithuanian Commonwealth against the Russian Empire. It began in 1863 and lasted until the last insurgents were captured in 1865.

SELECTED BIBLIOGRAPHY
OF WORKS IN ENGLISH

—

Brumfield, William C. "Bazarov and Rjazanov: The Romantic Archetype in Russian Nihilism." *Slavic and East European Journal* 21, no. 4 (Winter 1977): 495–505.

Brumfield, William C. "Sleptsov Redivus." In *California Slavic Studies*, vol. 9, 27–71. Berkeley, CA, 1976.

Freeborn, Richard. "Egotistical and Revolutionary Nihilism." In *The Russian Novel: Turgenev to Pasternak*, 29–30. Cambridge: Cambridge University Press, 1982.

Glickman, Rose. "An Alternative View of the Peasantry: The Raznochintsy Writers of the 1860s." *Slavic Review* 32, no. 4 (December 1973): 693–704.

Moser, Charles A. *Antinihilism in the Russian Novel of the 1860s.* The Hague: Mouton, 1964.

Offord, Derek. "Literature and Ideas in Russia after the Crimean War: The 'Plebian' Writers." In *Ideology in Russian Literature*, edited by Richard Freeborn and Jane Grayson, 68–78. New York: St. Martin's Press, 1990.

Rogachevskii, Andrei. "Precursors of Soviet Realism: Vasili Sleptsov's 'Trudnoe vremya' and Its Anti-Nihilist Opponents." *Slavonic and East European Review* 75, no. 1 (January 1997): 36–62.